This book belongs

Grace!

CONTRIBUTORS

Illustrated by
Alison Atkins, Andrew Geeson, Andy Everitt Stewart,
Anglea Kincaid, Anna Cynthia Leplar, Caroline Davis,
Claire Henley, Claire Mumford, Daniel Howarth,
Dorothy Clark, Elaine Keary, Frank Endersby,
Georgia Birkett, Gillian Roberts, Jacqueline East,
Jacqueline Mair, Jan Lewis, Jane Molineaux,
Jane Swift, Jane Tattersfield, Jessica Stockham,
Jo Brown, Julie Nicholson, Karen Perrins, Kate Aldous,
Kate Davies, Linda Worrell, Liz Pichon, Louise Gardner,
Maggie Downer, Mario Capaldi, Martin Grant, Nicola Evans,
Paula Martyr, Peter Rutherford, Piers Harper, Rebecca Elgar,
Rikki O'Neill, Rory Tyger, Sara Walker, Scott Rhodes,
Serena Feneziani, Sheila Moxley, Stephanie Boey, Sue Clarke,
Terry Burton, Pauline Siewart, Lorna Bannister

Written by
Nicola Baxter, Janet Allison Brown, Andrew Charman, Jillian
Harker, Heather Henning, Alistair Hedley, Claire Keen,
Ronne Randall, Lesley Rees, Caroline Repchuk, Kay Barnes,
Gaby Goldsack, Aneurin Rhys, Louisa Somerville, Derek Hall,
Marilyn Tolhurst, Alison Morris, Nicola Edwards,
Jackie Andrews

ANIMAL TALES

A Keepsake Treasury

Every effort has been made to acknowledge the
contributors to this book. If we have made any errors,
we will be pleased to rectify them in future editions.

This is a Parragon Book
This edition published in 2005

Parragon
Queen Street House
4 Queen Street
Bath BA1 1HE, UK

Design and project management by Aztec Design

Page make-up by Mik Martin and Caroline Reeves

ISBN 1-40544-632-3
Printed in China

ANIMAL TALES

A Keepsake Treasury

Contents

CONTENTS

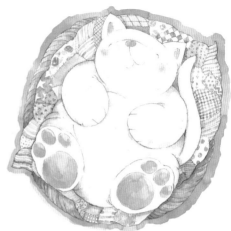

CONTENTS

Little
Chick
Lost

" Stay close, Little Chick!" said Mummy, as they set out to visit Mrs Duck, who lived on the pond. Little Chick tried to keep up with Mummy, but there were so many interesting things to look at that he soon got lost in the long grass.

He was busy amongst the toadstools watching a shiny beetle climb slowly up a stem of grass, when a dark shadow fell over him.

He looked up to see a huge mouth coming silently towards him! It was a fox, and he looked rather hungry!

"Help!" cried Little Chick, looking around for somewhere to hide.

Just then, Spot the farm dog appeared and with a great woof he chased the fox away. He was good at protecting the farm animals.

Mummy arrived flapping her wings. "I told you to stay close," she said, tucking Little Chick under her wing.

And from then on, that is just where Little Chick stayed!

Sports Day

The sun peeped over the higgledy-piggledy, messy alley. It was much too early to be awake – or was it? Lenny the kitten slowly opened his eyes and grinned – it was "time-to-get-up" time.

"Get up, Sleepyhead!" he yelled to his twin sister, Lulu. "It's a great day for running and jumping." And he started to run round and round the dustbins.

"Okay, Lenny," yawned Lulu, still half asleep, "I'm just coming."

"I'll race you to the end of the alley," cried Lenny.

"But you always win," moaned Lulu.

"That's because you're a big, podgy pussy," laughed Lenny.

Lulu giggled. "Cheeky kitty!" she cried. "Bet you can't catch me!" And she ran down the alley as fast as she could.

"That was fun!" cried Lenny, as he finally caught up with his sister. "What about some jumping now?"

"Great idea," purred Lulu.

So, huffing and puffing, the little kittens piled up some boxes and put a pole across the gap.

Lenny leapt over it first. "Whee!" he cried. "I bet I can jump higher than you!"

Suddenly, Lulu spotted a tatty old ball. "I bet I can throw it further than you!" she cried.

"No, you can't," cried Lenny. He picked up the ball and threw his best throw ever – but it hit Uncle Bertie right on the head!

Scampering down the alley as fast as they could go, the two kittens quickly hid behind a heap of old potato sacks before Uncle Bertie could spot them!

"Pooh!" said Lulu. "These sacks are really very smelly!"

Suddenly, Lenny had an idea...

Sticking his feet into one of the old potato sacks, he pulled it up to his tummy and began hopping and jumping around!

"Hey, what about a sack race?" he giggled.

Lenny hopped and skipped. Lulu wiggled and giggled.

"I'm winning!" squealed Lulu. "I'm winning!"

"No, you're not!" cried Lenny. He jumped his best jump ever – and knocked a huge pile of boxes over Cousin Archie!

"Uh-oh!" groaned Lenny. "Trouble time!"

Uncle Bertie and Cousin Archie were not happy. They stomped off to find Hattie, the kittens' mother.

"Those kittens of yours are so naughty," they complained. "You've got to do something about them!"

Hattie sighed. Then, spying two

pairs of tiny ears peeping out from behind a watering can, she tip-toed over. "Time-to-come-out-time!" she boomed.

"What have you two been up to?" Hattie asked Lenny and Lulu.

"Running and jumping, Mummy," whined Lenny.

"We didn't mean to hurt anyone," whispered Lulu. But Hattie wasn't cross. She knew her kittens were only playing.

"I've got an idea," she said. "Why don't we have a sports day? We can all join in – there'll be plenty of running and jumping for everyone!"

Archie and Bertie didn't want to play – they wanted a cat nap!

"Okay," said Hattie. "We'll simply ask the dogs to join us instead."

So, later that day, Hattie explained her idea to the Alley Dogs, who all thought it sounded like great fun. And it wasn't long before Hattie had organised everyone and everything!

"We'll have lots of races," cried Lenny, excitedly, "running, skipping, leaping and jumping ones – perhaps a sack race!"

Suddenly, six pussy eyes peeped over the fence.

"Okay, everyone," cried Hattie. "Let's begin. Ready... steady... "

"Er, Hattie," asked Cousin Archie, popping out from behind the fence, "can I join in?"

"Us too?" cried Uncle Bertie and Auntie Lucy.

"Of course you can," laughed Hattie.

"Ready... steady... GO!"

Cousin Archie and Harvey raced up the alley and passed the finishing line together. "Archie and Harvey are the winners!" cried Hattie. "Time for the sack race now!"

The dogs and cats all clambered into their sacks. But Lenny and Lulu began before Hattie could say "Go!"

"Hey!" cried Hattie. "Come back you two, that's cheating!" But it was too late. Everyone began leaping and jumping after the kittens.

"STOP!" shouted Hattie.

Lenny and Lulu stopped – but no one else did! They crashed into each other and fell in a big Alley Cat and Dog pickle!

Luckily, no one was hurt, but now they were all tired.

"Well, that was the best sports day ever!" said Harvey.

Hattie looked at the higgledy-piggledy mess.

"You're right," she laughed. "But tomorrow we're going to play another game. It's called tidy-up the alley!"

Suddenly, lots of barking and meowing filled the air. "Oh, no!" they groaned, and then they all laughed.

Custard's New Home

Custard the little hippo lived where it was very hot. His home was a cool river that flowed into the sea. Sid, the hermit crab, and Custard were best friends. This was a bit odd because they were as different as could be. Custard was a lot bigger than Sid for a start.

Custard thought that being a hermit crab must be really cool, they keep moving from one shell to another. At the moment Sid had a bright pink, pointed shell which he carried around everywhere he went. Custard wanted to carry his own home around with him! Then he wouldn't have to stay out in the hot sun. Hippos don't like getting hot. But there are no shells as big as a hippo. So they have to stay in the river to keep cool.

"Will you help me build my own home?" Custard asked Sid one day.

And so they built a house of leaves and they tied it to Custard's back. He was very pleased, and they went for a walk by the river to celebrate. Sid wore a new round blue shell this time.

They passed a lion that had a bad cold. "ATISHOO!"

The lion sneezed loudly and blew Custard's new house away! So they built a house of bamboo this time. "This won't blow away," said Custard.

But an elephant appeared. And, oh dear! Bamboo is an elephant's favourite food. "Yummy!" said the elephant. "Thanks for bringing me my breakfast!" And he stuffed Custard's house into his mouth!

Meanwhile, Sid was looking for another new home. But a large bird flying lazily overhead spotted Sid without his shell. "Ah, crab lunch!" it said, and, swooping down, grabbed Sid. But Sid wriggled until he was free.

Custard rushed to help, but he was so big and slow. Looking round, he spotted a deckchair, a sunshade and a bucket and spade. "Quick," he called to Sid, "over here!" Sid was just in time! Custard wriggled his bottom into the stripy deckchair, and settled down under the shade of the green umbrella. It felt nice and cool. If only his head and legs didn't stick out in front. He wriggled a bit more, trying to get comfortable.

"Sid, I've been thinking. I'll just keep cool in the river like I did before," said Custard.

"And I think I'll look for another shell," said Sid.

The two friends wandered back down to the river, happy to be going home together.

Trampling Trotters

Mrs MacDonald had a little garden near the farmhouse. She was usually very busy on the farm, but she always managed to find time to look after the flowers. But the hens also loved the flowers – for their own reasons!

"Marigolds are delicious," Henry would mutter, talking with his beak full as usual.

Mrs MacDonald watched the hens through the kitchen window. If they tip-toed into the garden, she would rush out, waving a tea towel.

"Shoo, you greedy birds!" she would call. "Leave my flowers alone!" And Henry and the hens would flutter away – for a while.

Early one morning, before Old MacDonald and Mrs MacDonald set off for the market, Mrs MacDonald had a word with the hens.

"There is plenty of grain in the henhouse," she said. "There is no need for you to go into my garden. Do you understand?"

The hens eagerly nodded and clucked but, whether this meant that they agreed or not, Mrs MacDonald wasn't quite sure.

As Old MacDonald's van disappeared down the lane, Henry the cockerel strutted towards a particularly beautiful clump of marigolds.

Jenny the hen scuttled anxiously after him. "Henry," she warned, "if we peck at those flowers, Mrs MacDonald is going to be very angry. Remember what happened last time!"

Henry was just thinking about those dreadful scenes when something large and pink dashed straight past him.

It was Percy the pig!

In his hurry, Old MacDonald had left the gate of the pigsty slightly open. Percy loved to have a run around the farmyard, and now he was heading for Mrs MacDonald's lovely garden.

That naughty pig rolled over and over on the flower beds. He rooted under the begonias. He jumped on to the marigolds. The garden was in a terrible mess!

"Are you thinking what I'm thinking?" asked Henry glumly.

"Yes," gulped the hens, looking at each other, and feeling very worried and sad. "Mrs MacDonald will think it was us!"

Now, usually hens are not known for being any good at hard work, but Jenny, Henrietta, Mary, Victoria and Henry all worked very hard.

They propped up the squashed flowers and stamped down the uprooted earth. They tried hard to clear up all the mess Percy made with his trampling trotters. But, when they heard the sound of Old MacDonald's van coming down the lane, the garden still looked a sorry sight. There was no way that the hens could disguise Percy's mess and destruction. Henry and the hens had done their best, but the garden was ruined.

Mrs MacDonald got out of the car and walked towards the farmhouse. But as she got closer she realised that something had happened. The fact that the hens and Henry were lined up beside the garden, shifting nervously from foot to foot made her rather suspicious. And then there was a long silence as Mrs MacDonald surveyed the scene. The hens and Henry became more and more worried as Mrs MacDonald walked all round the garden, surveying the damage.

Finally, Mrs MacDonald said, "Don't worry, ladies, and don't worry, Henry. It is obvious that someone bigger and bulkier than any of you has been bouncing in my begonias, trampling on my daisies and digging holes in my flower beds! I think that we shall all have a special snack, and then I shall have a sit down before deciding how to deal with that pig!"

Henry and the hens all sighed with relief, for once they weren't to blame!

The Smiley Crocodile

Open-wide was the friendliest crocodile for miles around. While all the grumpy crocodiles were snapping and snarling and being very cross, Open-wide grinned at everyone. He had a very, very big smile. "You smile too much," the others told him. "Be fierce… like a real crocodile!"

"I'll try," said Open-wide, and he put on a scowly face. It lasted two seconds and then the smile came back again.

One day, some hippos came to the river. They were very large and there were a lot of them. They waded into the part of the river that the crocodiles liked the best. Open-wide liked to watch them when they sank to the bottom and then came up very slowly making lots of ripples. He liked it when they blew fountains of water up into the air. The grumpy crocodiles didn't like it one little bit!

Open-wide saw a baby hippo called Sausage playing in the water. "Look, I bet you can't do this!" said Sausage to Open-wide, and he blew a million bubbles so that they floated in a cloud across the top of the water.

"I bet that I can," said Open-wide. And he did… through his nose!

They played all day... and every day after that! Open-wide had never had such a good time.

The grumpy crocodiles tried to think of ways to get rid of the hippos. First they tried to be frightening by showing lots of teeth. The hippos just smiled... and showed even bigger teeth! Next they charged the hippos while they were swimming. The hippos sank to the bottom of the river where it was too deep for the crocodiles.

The crocodiles didn't know what else to do. Open-wide had an idea! "Why don't I just smile at them and ask nicely if they will move?" he said.

"Pooh!" said the crocodiles. "Fat lot of good that will do! Oh, go on then," said the grumpy crocodiles, "but it won't work, you'll see."

But it did! The hippos liked Open-wide; he had a big smile just like them. They listened politely when he explained that the crocodiles didn't really like fun. They would rather be on their own and grumpy.

"We'll move further down the river if you will still come and play with Sausage," they said. And that's what happened.

The crocodiles were amazed! They didn't say anything to Open-wide, but they did wonder if smiling was better than scowling after all!

Barking Night

It was the middle of the night. Harvey and his gang were fast asleep in the higgledy-piggledy, messy alley, dreaming of yummy bones and chasing dustmen! The only sounds were the gentle rumblings of Ruffles' tummy and Bonnie's snores!

Everyone and everything was fast asleep – or were they? Six naughty Alley Cats peeped over the fence. They spied the snoozing dogs and, grinning and sniggering, they scribbled and scrabbled up the fence.

"I've got an idea!" whispered Archie. "Listen… "

Wibbling and wobbling, the Alley Cats stood in a line along the top of the fence…

"Those dippy dogs are in for a fright!" giggled Archie.

"I bet I'll be the loudest!" boasted Lenny.

The cats took a deep breath, and out came the scariest, screechiest sounds you ever heard!

The terrible noise woke Harvey with a start and made him fall off his mattress, straight on to Mac!

"What's that noise?" yelped Mac. "Is it the bagpipe ghost?"

"G-Ghost?" cried Puddles, rushing up to Harvey. "Help!"

The noise made Patchy and Ruffles jump. They fell in a big heap on top of Ruffles' bed!

"Save us!" they cried.

Harvey spotted the culprits. "Oh, it's just those pesky pussies," he groaned, "up to mischief again. Don't worry, everyone, let's just ignore them and go back to sleep."

But those naughty cats weren't finished yet!

"Look!" cried Lenny. "One of them is still asleep. We must try harder."

They were right – Bonnie was still snoring in her dustbin!

"Louder! Louder!" screeched Archie to the others. But could they wake Bonnie? Oh no! She just kept on snoring and snoring and... snoring!

"I think someone should teach those cats a lesson," growled Mac. "When I was a pup I'd... "

"Not now, Mac!" shouted the others.

Harvey smiled. He had an idea. The gang huddled together and listened as Harvey told them his idea.

"And me! And me!" cried Puddles, squeezing herself in.

The cats thought they were so clever. They laughed and then they wailed even louder than before!

Then suddenly, Lenny slipped and grabbed Lulu, who grabbed Hattie, who grabbed Bertie, who grabbed Lucy, who grabbed Archie – and they all tumbled headfirst into the pile of boxes and bins!

"Bravo!" woofed the dogs. "More! More!" The cats squealed and wailed and ran away. They'd had enough of playing tricks for one day!

"Now to get our own back," chuckled Harvey. The gang sneaked along the alley as quiet as little mice.

"Ready?" whispered Harvey. "Steady – GO!"

"WOOF! WOOF!"

The ground shook and the cats jumped high into the air.

"Ha-ha!" roared the dogs. "Scaredy-cats! Scaredy-cats! We've got our own back! I think that's enough frights for one night!" said Harvey.

"You're right," agreed Archie, sheepishly. "Let's go back to bed. No more tricks tonight."

Just then Bonnie woke up. "Is it 'time-to-get-up' time?" she asked, rubbing her eyes.

"No!" said Patchy, "it's 'time-for-bed' time!" and they all laughed and laughed.

"Oh, goody!" yawned Bonnie. "Bedtime! The best time of the day!"

"Oh, Bonnie," smiled Harvey. "What a sleepyhead you are!"

But Bonnie didn't care. With another enormous yawn and a stretch, she turned away and wandered back to her dustbin – she was soooo tired!

At last the cats and dogs of the higgledy-piggledy, messy alley snuggled down to sleep, dreaming of yummy bones and chasing dustbin men – and lots of bowls of scrummy fish!

The only sounds were the gentle rumblings of Ruffles' tummy and Bonnie's snores.

Everyone and everything was fast asleep – or were they?

"TOO WHIT TOOWHOOOOOOO!"

"TOO WHIT TOOWHOOOOOOO!"

Lion

It was Lion's birthday.
"The animals must have forgotten," said Lion. "No one has wished me happy birthday."

Lion walked slowly through the jungle, feeling very sad.

"Let's surprise Lion with a birthday party!" said Elephant.

"We'll bring our birthday presents," said Giraffe…

"…and we will think of lots of games to play," said Monkey.

"We'll dance and have fun," said Zebra.

"HAPPY BIRTHDAY, LION!" called Hippo.

"Happy birthday!" sang the animals.

"What a SURPRISE!" roared Lion.

Monkey

Tiny Monkey looked sad. He did not know how to climb. The animals decided they would try to cheer him up.

"I'll bring some leaves to shade you from the sun," said Giraffe.

"I will bring feathers to make a cosy bed for you," said Parrot.

"And a long bedtime story will help you to sleep," yawned Lion.

"But I don't want to sleep," said Tiny Monkey. "I want to learn to climb."

"I will teach you, Tiny Monkey," said Big Monkey.

"Just follow me. Cling with your feet, and swing your tail – like this!"

Taking a deep breath, Tiny Monkey raced up the tree, clinging to the branches.

"Look at me! I'm the best climbing monkey in the forest!" he called.

The Disappearing Eggs

Mrs Hen had been sitting on her nest for a long time, and she was tired and uncomfortable. "I wish these eggs would hurry up and hatch!" she said to herself, crossly. But all she could do was sit and wait, so she closed her eyes and soon fell fast asleep.

She dreamt she was sitting on her nest when all of a sudden it started to wobble and shake. She was tipped this way, and that, being poked and prodded as the eggs moved beneath her – someone was stealing her eggs!

Mrs Hen woke with a start, and looked down at her nest in alarm. Sure enough, her eggs had disappeared – but in their place were six fluffy chicks, all prodding her with their sharp little beaks.

"What lovely big chicks!" said a deep voice nearby. It was Old Ned the donkey.

"Yes!" said Mrs Hen with relief. "They were really worth the wait!"

Hippo's Holiday

It was a warm, sunny morning in the jungle. "A perfect time for a long, relaxing wallow," thought Howard Hippo.
Wallowing in the river was Howard's favourite thing to do. He found a nice, cool, muddy spot and settled in. Howard was just drifting off into a delightful daydream, when... SPLASH! "Gotcha!" shrieked Maxine Monkey. SPLOOSH! "Gotcha back!" shouted Chico Chimp.

"Can't you monkeys and chimps play somewhere else?" Howard grumbled. "I'm wallowing here!"

"Oops! Sorry, Howard," Maxine apologised. But it was too late. Howard's wallow was ruined.

That afternoon, as the hot sun beat down on his back, Howard slithered into the river to cool off.

"Aaah," he breathed happily, as he soaked in the cool water. "This is sooo lovely."

"Yoo-hoo! Howard!" called Penelope Parrot. "I've just learned to do a double-rollover-loop-the-loop! Want to see?"

"Sure, Penelope," sighed Howard. It didn't look as if he was going to have a chance to relax this afternoon, either!

The next morning, Howard's cousin, Hilary, came to visit.

"You look exhausted, Howard," she said.

"That's because I never have a chance to relax and wallow any more," said Howard.

"What you need is a holiday. I'm leaving for Hippo Hollow this afternoon. Why don't you come with me? You would love Hippo Hollow," said Hilary, as the two hippos trundled through the jungle. "There are lots of great, big waterfalls!" continued Hilary.

Howard imagined having lots of long, cool showers.

"And there's so much mud!"

Howard saw himself relaxing in a cool mud bath.

"And everyone has lots and lots of FUN!" finished Hilary.

Howard thought about playing games with new hippo friends.
He agreed with Hilary that it sounded a very good idea, and they set off
through the jungle.

At last Howard and Hilary arrived at Hippo Hollow.

"It's even more beautiful than I had imagined!" Howard
exclaimed. "And it looks like we've arrived just in time!" said Hilary.

"For what?" asked Howard. "A relaxing mud bath?"

"No, silly!" laughed Hilary. "Hippo-robics!"

"Let's get moving, everyone!" called a sleek-looking hippo.
Lots of other hippos galloped into the stream behind her.

"Come on, Howard," said Hilary. "Don't be a
party pooper on the first day of your holiday!"

Howard had no choice but to join in. One,
two, three, four! Kick, two, three, four!"
shouted the instructor.

Howard did his best and kicked with all the
others. "Surely everyone will want a nice, long

rest after all this exercise?" he thought. But he was wrong! After a quick shower in the waterfall, everyone rushed off to play Volley-Melon and Hilary wanted Howard on her team. Howard finally did get to have a rest after lunch – but not for long!

"You're looking much more relaxed, Howard," Hilary called, as she led her junior swimming class right past him. "This holiday was just what you needed, wasn't it?"

"Er… I guess so," Howard replied, weakly. After his busy day, Howard was hoping for an early night. He was just getting settled, when he heard Hilary.

"Come on, Howard!" she bellowed. "You don't want to miss the Hippo-Hooray Cabaret! They are so good!"

"Oh – YAWN – that sounds wonderful," sighed Howard, with a yawn. He could barely keep his eyes open.

The next morning, Howard was sliding into the river, when he heard Hilary calling.

"Is it time for Hippo-robics?" he asked.

"Oh, no," said Hilary. "I think that what you need is lots of good, fresh air. So we're going on a hike!"

Howard huffed and puffed all through the exhausting hike.

"I hope I can have a lovely, long, cool bath when this is over," he thought. Howard got his wish. But, as he was soaking his sore muscles, Hilary came by for a chat.

"The hike was fun, wasn't it?" she said.

"Oh yes," said Howard. "In fact, I enjoyed it so much, that I've decided to go on another one!"

"Really?" said Hilary. "That's great! Where are you hiking to?"

"Home!" said Howard. "I'm going home, where I can have a REAL holiday. And where there are no Hippo-robics, and no Volley-Melon games, no cabarets and no one to stop me wallowing as long as I like!"

And so that's exactly what Howard did!

Kiss It Better

Rumpus was romping around the living room. He cartwheeled across the carpet. He turned a somersault on the sofa. "Be careful!" called Mum. Too late! Rumpus slipped from the sofa, crumpled on to the carpet and banged his head on the floor. "My head hurts!" he groaned.

"Come here and I'll kiss it better," said Mum. She hugged Rumpus and planted a kiss on his forehead. "Now, go and find something less rowdy to do," she said.

Rumpus rushed out into the garden and began to ride his bike. Round and round he raced. "Watch out!" called Mum.

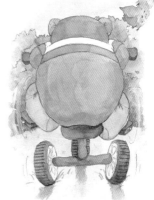

Too late! Rumpus crashed into the corner of the wheelbarrow and tumbled to the ground and grazed his knee. "My leg hurts!" he wailed.

"Come here and I'll kiss it better," said Mum. She hugged Rumpus and planted a kiss on his knee.

"Now, go and find something safer to do," she said. Rumpus ran up the grassy slope. Then he rolled down. "Roly poly, down the hill," he sang. "Look where you're going!" called Mum.

Too late! Rumpus rolled right into the rose bush. The thorns scratched him all along his arm. "My arm's sore!" cried Rumpus.

"Come here and I'll kiss it better," said Mum and she planted kisses all up his arm.

Mum went into the kitchen. "I need a break," she thought. She made a cup of tea. She cut herself a slice of cake. Then, she sat down for five minutes. Just as she picked up her cup, Rumpus zoomed into the kitchen on his skateboard.

"Rumpus!" said Mum. "Can't you find something more sensible to do?" Mum moved into the living room. "I need a rest," she thought. She sat down on the sofa and picked up the paper.

"Boom! Boom! Boom!" In marched Rumpus, banging on his drum. Mum sighed a loud sigh. "Is anything wrong?" asked Rumpus.

"I've got a headache!" said Mum.

"Never mind," smiled Rumpus, throwing his arms around her. "I'll soon kiss it better."

The Littlest Pig

Little Pig had a secret. He snuggled down
in the warm hay with his brothers and sisters, looked up at the dark
sky twinkling with stars, and smiled a secret smile to himself. Maybe it
wasn't so bad being the littlest pig after all...

Not so long ago, Little Pig had been feeling quite fed up. He was the
youngest and by far the smallest pig in the family. He had five brothers
and five sisters and they were all much bigger and fatter than he was. The
farmer's wife called him Runt, as he was the smallest pig of the litter.

"I don't suppose little Runt will come to much," she told her friend
Daisy, as they stopped by to bring the piglets some fresh hay.

His brothers and sisters teased him terribly. "Poor little Runtie," they
said to him, giggling. "You must be the smallest pig in the world! We are
all much bigger and stronger than you!"

"Leave me alone! Why are you all so horrible to me? I haven't done
anything to any of you!" said Little Pig, sadly, and he crept off to the
corner of the pigpen, where he curled into a ball, and started to cry.
"If they weren't all so nasty and greedy, and they let me have some food

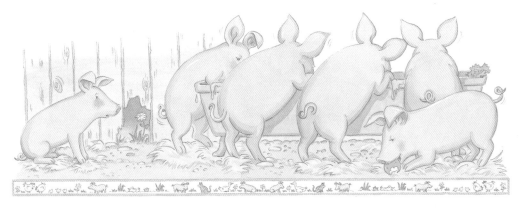

instead of pushing me out of the way, maybe I would be bigger!" he mumbled to himself.

But every feeding time was the same – the others all pushed and shoved, and shunted Little Pig out of the way, until all that was left was the scraps. He would never grow bigger at this rate.

Then one day Little Pig made an important discovery. He was hiding in the corner of the pen, as usual, when he spied a little hole in the fence tucked away behind the feeding trough.

"I think I could fit through there!" thought Little Pig, excitedly.

He waited all day until it was time for bed, and then, when he was sure that all of his brothers and sisters were fast asleep, he wriggled through the hole. Suddenly he was outside, free to go wherever he pleased.

And what an adventure he had!

First, he ran to the hen house and gobbled up the bowls of grain that had been left for the hens' breakfast.

Then he ran to the field, slipped under the fence, and crunched up all of Donkey's carrots.

Then he ran into the vegetable patch and munched a whole row

of juicy green cabbages. He licked his lips in delight – what a feast!

Then, when his little belly was full to bursting, he headed for home. On the way he stopped by the hedgerow. What was that lovely smell? He rooted around until he found where it was coming from – it was a big bank of luscious wild strawberries.

Little Pig had never tasted anything so delicious!

"I think that tomorrow night, I shall start with these!" he promised himself as he trotted back home to the pigpen.

Quietly he wriggled back through the hole, and soon fell fast asleep snuggled up to his mother, smiling contentedly.

Night after night Little Pig continued his tasty adventures, quietly creeping out through the hole while all his brothers and sisters were sleeping. He no longer minded when they pushed him out of the way at feeding time, as he knew a much better feast awaited him outside. The others didn't notice that their little brother was smiling all day, and no longer got upset when they were rude to him.

Sometimes he would find the farm dog's bowl filled with scraps from the farmer's supper, or buckets of oats ready for the horses. "Yum, yum –

piggy porridge!" he would giggle, as he gobbled it up.

But as the days and weeks went by, and Little Pig grew bigger and fatter, it was more of a squeeze to wriggle through the hole each night.

Little Pig knew that soon he would no longer be able to fit through the hole, but by then he would be big enough to stand up to his brothers and sisters. And for now he was enjoying his secret!

Elephant

Here is Baby Elephant. Baby Elephant plays with his friends, and he helps them, too.

"Giraffe, you've lost your patterns in the mud," said Baby Elephant. "I'll spray you with my trunk."

"Lion, you look too hot," said Baby Elephant. "I'll shade you with my big ears."

"Monkey, you look very tired," said Baby Elephant. "I'll carry you on my back."

"Oh no. Rhino! You've fallen in the river," said Baby Elephant. "Hold on to my tail very tightly, and I will pull you out."

After his hard work helping his friends, Baby Elephant decided to have a rest under a tree.

"We'll all stay close to Baby Elephant," said his friends, "to make sure he is safe while he rests."

Tiger

Baby Tiger lived in the jungle. One day he fell fast asleep, and his friends could not find him.

"Where is Baby Tiger?" they asked.

Monkey climbed to the top of the highest tree. Rhino ran fast along the riverbank. Elephant searched deep in the jungle.

"Where are you, Baby Tiger?" they called, as loudly as they could.

Then Elephant gave such a loud trumpet that Baby Tiger was woken up.

"Here I am," called Baby Tiger, and with a sleepy yawn and a stretch he waved a stripy paw.

"Baby Tiger! We've been looking everywhere for you," said the animals.

"We couldn't see you because of your stripes," said Monkey.

"We missed you, Baby Tiger," they said, giving him a great big hug.

Cheeky Chick

Cheeky Chick was a playful little chick. He was always playing tricks on his brothers and sisters. He would hide in the long grass, then jump out on them in surprise, shouting, "Boo!"

One day they decided to get their own back. "Let's play hide and seek," they said. They left Cheeky Chick to count to ten, while they all went to hide. Cheeky Chick hunted high and low for his brothers and sisters in all his favourite hiding places but they were nowhere to be found.

"Come out," he called. "I give up!" But no one came.

So Cheeky Chick carried on looking. He searched carefully all over the farmyard, in the vegetable patch and in the empty flower pots. He looked along the hedgerow. He even looked in the haystack, which took a very long time, but there was no sign of his brothers and sisters to be found amongst the hay. By now it was getting dark, and Cheeky Chick was feeling scared and lonely. He decided to go home.

He hurried to the henhouse and opened the door. "Surprise!" came a loud chorus. His brothers and sisters had been hiding there all along! It was a long time before Cheeky Chick played tricks on them again.

Greedy Bear

If there is one thing in the whole wide world that a teddy bear likes more than anything, it is buns – big sticky currant buns with sugary tops, and squishy middles.

A teddy bear will do almost anything for a bun. But for one greedy little teddy bear called Clarence, sticky buns were to be his unsticking!

Rag Doll baked the most wonderful buns in the little toy cooker. She baked big buns and small buns, iced buns and currant buns, Bath buns and cream buns, and even hot cross buns! She shared them out amongst the toys in the playroom, and everybody loved them. But no one loved them as much as Clarence.

"If you will give me your bun, I'll polish your boots!" he'd say to Tin Soldier.

And sometimes, if Tin Soldier was not feeling too hungry, he'd agree. There was always someone who would give Clarence their bun in return for a favour, and sometimes Clarence would eat five or six buns in one day!

Then he'd be busy washing the dolls' dresses, or brushing Scotty Dog's fur. He would even stand still and let the clown throw custard pies at him!

So you see, Clarence was not a lazy bear, but he was a greedy bear, and in spite of all his busyness, he was becoming a rather plump little greedy bear. All those buns were starting to show around his middle, and his fur was beginning to strain at the seams!

Then one day Clarence rushed into the playroom full of excitement. His owner, Penny, had told him that next week she was taking him on a teddy bears' picnic with lots of other teddy bears. "She says there will be honey sandwiches and ice cream and biscuits – and lots and lots of buns!" Clarence told the others, rubbing his paws together. "I can hardly wait!

In fact all this excitement has made me hungry, so I think I'll have a bun." And he took a big sticky bun out from under a cushion where he'd hidden it earlier.

"Oh, Clarence!" said Rabbit. "You know, one of these days you will simply go pop!"

"Just be happy I don't like carrots!" said Clarence, with a smile.

Well, that week Clarence was busier than ever. Every time he thought about the picnic he felt hungry, and then he'd have to find someone who'd let him have their bun. He ate bun after bun, and would not listen when Rag Doll warned him that his back seam was starting to come undone.

The day of the teddy bears' picnic dawned, and Clarence yawned and stretched, smiling with excitement. But as he stretched he felt a popping sensation all down his stomach. He tried to sit up in bed, but to his alarm he found he could not move. Very slowly, he looked down his front.

To his dismay, he saw that the seams around his tummy had popped open, and his stuffing was spilling out all over the bed!

"Help me!" he cried. "I seem to be exploding!"

Just then, Penny woke up. "Oh, Clarence!" she cried when she saw him. "I can't take you to the teddy bears' picnic like that!"

Penny showed Clarence to her mummy, who said he would have to go to the toy hospital.

Clarence was away from the playroom for a whole week, but when he came back he was as good as new. Some of his stuffing had been taken out, and he was all sewn up again.

He had had lots of time to think in the hospital about what a silly greedy bear he had been. How he wished he had not missed the picnic. The other teddies said it was the best day out they had ever had. Penny had taken Rabbit instead.

"It was terrible," moaned Rabbit. "Not a carrot in sight. I did save you a bun though." And he pulled a big sticky bun out of his pocket.

"No thank you, Rabbit," said Clarence. "I've gone off buns!"

Of course, Clarence did not stop eating buns for long, but from then on he stuck to one a day. And he still did favours for the others, only now he did them for free!

Fierce Tiger

Tiger wasn't really a tiger. He was a fierce stray kitten. People called him Tiger because he hissed and arched his back whenever they came near. Tiger didn't trust people. If they came too near, he would show his claws and even scratch them. At night he wandered the streets, searching dustbins for scraps and stealing food put out for pets. During the day, he slept wherever he could.

One cold winter's night, Tiger was wandering the streets when it began to snow. He spotted an open window.

"Aha," thought Tiger. "I bet it's warm and dry in there." He jumped in and found himself in a dark porch. He curled into a ball and was soon fast asleep. He was so comfortable that he slept all through the night. When he finally awoke, there was no one around. But beside him were a bowl of food and a dish of water.

"Don't mind if I do," purred Tiger. He gobbled it all down, then drank some water before leaving through the window again. The day was colder than any Tiger had ever known so, when he saw the window open that night, he sneaked in.

This time Tiger noticed the door from the porch was ajar. He pushed it open and found a warm kitchen – so he settled down and had a wonderful night's sleep. When he awoke in the morning, he found a bowl of delicious fish and a dish of water beside him. "Don't mind if I do," purred Tiger as he wolfed it all down before he left.

That night it was still snowing. Tiger went back, and this time he found a basket by the fire. "Don't mind if I do," purred Tiger as he crawled in and went to sleep. In the morning, Tiger heard a rattling sound. He opened one eye. A little boy was putting a bowl by the basket. Tiger stared at the little boy. The little boy stared at Tiger.

"Good boy," whispered the little boy, gently.

Tiger looked at the bowl. It was full of milk. "Don't mind if I do," he purred, and he drank the lot.

After that, Tiger returned to the house every night, and soon he never slept anywhere else. The little boy always gave him plenty to eat and drink. And, in return, Tiger let the little boy stroke him and hold him on his lap.

Tiger was no longer a fierce stray kitten!

Whale Song

"Oh, what a beautiful morning!" sang Flippy the whale, as streaks of sunlight filtered down through the clear, blue ocean. He swam to and fro, twirled around, then whooshed up through the waves, and jumped clear of the water in a perfect pirouette.

Flippy loved to sing and dance. The trouble was, although he was a very graceful dancer, his singing was terrible. His big mouth would open

wide, as he boomed out song after song – but none of them were in tune! The dreadful sound echoed through the ocean for miles, sending all the fish and other ocean creatures diving into the rocks and reefs for cover, as the waters shook around them. It was always worse when the sun shone, as the bright warm sun made Flippy want to sing and dance with happiness. It had got so bad that the other creatures had begun to pray for dull skies and rain.

"Something has got to be done!" complained Wobble the jellyfish. "Flippy's booming voice makes me quiver and shake so much that I can't see where I'm going!"

"Well, I know where I'm going," said Snappy the lobster. "As far away as possible. My head is splitting from Flippy's awful wailing."

"Someone will have to tell Flippy not to sing any more," said Sparky the stingray.

"But it will hurt his feelings," said Wobble.

"Not as much as his singing hurts my ears!" snapped Snappy.

And so they decided that Sparky would tell Flippy the next day that they did not want him to sing any more songs. Wobble was right.

Flippy was very upset when he heard that the others did not like his singing. He cried big, salty tears.

"I was only trying to enjoy myself!" he sobbed. "I didn't realise I was upsetting everyone else."

"There, there," said Sparky, wishing he had not been chosen to give the little whale the bad news. "You can still enjoy dancing."

"It's not the same without music," said Flippy, miserably. "You can't get the rhythm." And he swam off into the deep waters, saying he wanted to be alone for a while.

As Flippy lay on the bottom of the ocean floor, feeling very sorry for himself, a beautiful sound came floating through the water from far away in the distance. It sounded like someone singing. Flippy wanted to know who was making such a lovely sound so, with a flick of his big tail, he set off in the direction it was coming from.

As he got closer, he could hear a soft voice singing a beautiful melody. Peering out from behind a big rock, he saw that the voice belonged to a little octopus, who was shuffling and swaying about on the ocean floor. His legs seemed to be going in all directions, as he stumbled and tripped along. Then he tried to spin around, but his legs got tangled and he crashed to the ground in a heap.

"Oh, dear," said Leggy the octopus. "I seem to have eight left feet!"

Flippy looked out shyly from behind the rock.

"What are you trying to do?" he asked.

The little octopus looked rather embarrassed.

"I was trying to dance," he said, blushing pink. "Only I'm not very good at it."

"Well, maybe I could teach you to dance," said Flippy. "I'm a very good dancer. And then, in return, there is something that I would love you to teach me!"

A few weeks later, Wobble, Snappy and Sparky were discussing how they missed having Flippy around, when they heard a strange and beautiful sound floating towards them through the ocean.

"Oh, what a beautiful morning... " came the song, only this time there were two voices singing in perfect harmony!

"Surely that can't be Flippy!" said the others in surprise.

But to their amazement, as the voices came closer they saw that, sure enough, it was Flippy, spinning and twirling as he danced gracefully towards them with his new friend!

On My Own

Deep in the jungle, where only wild things go, Mungo's mum was teaching him what a young monkey needs to know. "Some things just aren't safe to try alone," she said.

"Why not?" said Mungo. "I'm big enough to do things – on my own!"

"Now Mungo," said Mum, "listen carefully, please. Did you hear what I said? Do you understand?"

"It's okay, Mum. I won't slip or fall. I can swing across there with no trouble at all," said Mungo. "I'm big enough to do it – on my own!"

"Now, we're going to cross the river using these stones," said Mum. "And, Mungo, don't do this alone."

"But Mum," said Mungo, and he ran on without stopping, "I'm really good at jumping and hopping. I'm big enough to do it – on my own!" And off he sprang!

"That Mungo trampled on my nose!" said Croc. "Next time, I'll nibble off his toes!"

And did Mungo hear poor old Croc groan? No!

Mungo smiled. "I said I could do it on my own!"

"Mungo," said Mum, with a serious look on her face, "the jungle can be a dangerous place. There are all sorts of corners for creatures to hide, so, from here on, make sure that you stay by my side."

"Oh, Mum," said Mungo, "I don't need to wait for you. I can easily find my own way through. I'm big enough to do it – on my own!"

Mungo thwacked Lion's nose as he sped past. "Ouch! That Mungo's so careless!" Lion said. Did Mungo hear poor old Lion groan? No! Mungo just grinned. "I told you I could do it – on my own."

"I think I've had enough for one day," Mum said. "Off you go, little monkey! It's time for bed!" It was Mungo's turn to let out a groan.

"I don't want to go to bed – on my own!"

"Well, kiss me goodnight, and I'll hold you and cuddle you tight," said Mum.

Lion roared, "Is that Mungo still awake?"

"Yes!" snapped Crocodile.

"Let's help him go to sleep," hissed Snake.

And into the velvety, starry sky drifted the sounds of a jungle lullaby.

Snowy and Blowy

Old MacDonald peered out of his window and decided to put on three extra jumpers.

"That's very sensible," said Mrs MacDonald. "You need to keep warm when it's snowy."

"What worries me," said Old MacDonald, "is that it's snowy and blowy. I must make sure that the sheep are safe. They really don't like it when the snow gets blown into heaps in the fields. I think that it's time we brought them down from the meadow, now that it is so cold."

Old MacDonald puffed and panted as he put on his boots and set off to trek through the snowy meadow, taking Bruce the sheepdog with him.

But when they both reached the meadow, none of the sheep were anywhere to be seen. They were completely hidden by the snow!

"On days like these," said Old MacDonald, "I wish I had black sheep instead of white ones."

Suddenly, Bruce started to behave in a very strange way, jumping up and down with his paws together, just like sheep do! Old MacDonald understood straight away. He laughed and patted Bruce's head. Then he shouted, "Today there is going to be a jumping competition to try to keep us all warm!

I think the rabbits in the next field will win, they are so good at jumping!"

There was a moment of silence, and then – woosh! One energetic sheep jumped up, making a great shower of snow all around. And then woosh! woosh! Two more sheep leapt into the air, shaking the snow from their coats. And in a moment the field was full of leaping, jumping sheep! Old MacDonald and Bruce stood and smiled as the sheep appeared from all corners of the meadow.

The sheep were determined to make quite sure that the rabbits in the next field didn't stand a chance. In fact, the rabbits were all snugly sleeping in their burrows, quite unaware that their honour as jumpers was at stake. Well, no sensible rabbit would be hopping about in weather like that, would they? Not when they could stay warm in their burrows!

Back in the farmyard, the other animals saw how warm and happy all the woolly jumpers were. Before long, everyone was joining in – much to the embarassment of the hens! The whole farmyard was full of laughing, smiling animals who were all jumping up and down – a very strange sight indeed!

Of course, Old MacDonald didn't join in. He was too busy puffing and panting again, trying to get his boots off. Mrs MacDonald was trying to stop the snow from his boots going all over her clean kitchen floor. In the end, she had to help him pull off his boots, and poor Old MacDonald's

toes were as icy as the snow outside! All he wanted to do was to settle
down in the warmth of the farmhouse and sit by the fire. And he could
smell his lunch,
which was making
his mouth water.
All that walking in
the wind and the
snow had made
him very hungry!

And of course
Bruce was too
busy thinking
about his bone to
stay out in the
yard with all those
bouncing animals.
His empty tummy
was far more
important! And
after all that
very energetic
bouncing, he was
looking forward
to sleeping by the
fire too.

Bunny Tails

Bunnies come in all different colours and sizes. Some have long ears and some have floppy ears. But all bunnies have fluffy tails. All except Alfie, that is. He had no tail at all and his friends teased him badly.

"Never mind, dear," said his mummy. "I love you, tail or no tail."

But Alfie did mind and at night he cried himself to sleep. Then one night he dreamt he met a fairy and told her all about his problem.

"A little fairy magic will soon fix that!" said the fairy. She took some dandelion clocks and sewed them together to make a lovely fluffy tail. "Turn around!" she said and fixed it in place in a flash.

Alfie woke with a start.

"If only my dream could come true," he thought sadly and looked down at his back. And there, to his amazement, was a fine fluffy white tail!

"I'm a real bunny at last!" he said proudly, running off to show his new tail to his friends.

Nibbling Neighbours

O ne sunny morning in the meadow, Annabel was happily munching away when she was surprised to discover a hole where there should be grass. "My dears," she mooed, "there's a hole in our field!"

There was no doubt about it. Someone had dug a round, deep hole in the ground.

"We must be careful not to fall into it," said Poppy, anxiously.

But the next morning, where there had been one hole before, now there were five!

"If this goes on," said Poppy, "we'll have nowhere to stand at all!"

"And nothing to eat," added Emily, sounding very alarmed.

By the end of the week, there were over a hundred holes all over the meadow.

"You've got some nibbling neighbours," said Old MacDonald. "It looks like a family of rabbits has come to stay."

The cows shuddered. "Those hopping things with long ears?" asked Heather. "I can't look my best with them around!"

"And they have very, very large families," warned Emily. "Not just one baby at a time, like cows do."

"It's odd we've never seen one," said Poppy thoughtfully. "Maybe they do their digging in the dark. I'm going to keep watch tonight."

That night, as the full moon rose over the meadow, Poppy pretended to fall asleep.

Although she was expecting it, she was shocked when two bright little eyes and a twitchy nose popped up right in front of her.

"Aaaaaghh!" cried Poppy.

"Aaaaaghh!" cried the rabbit, and then disappeared down its hole as fast as it had appeared.

"You should have followed it!" cried Annabel, who had been woken by the sudden noises.

"Down a rabbit hole?" gasped Emily. "Don't be so silly, Annabel. She's far too big! How did you think a cow was going to get down a rabbit hole?"

"Then we're doomed," said Heather, gloomily. "Those rabbits will take over without us even seeing them do it."

The next morning, the cows awoke to an amazing sight. Hundreds of rabbits were sitting all around them.

"Excuse me!" said the largest one. "We have come to ask for your help. Please could we talk to you?"

"Help?" echoed Annabel. "We're the ones who need help!"

Then the rabbit explained that his family were very afraid. "We are worried because your hooves are so big, you could stamp on us without noticing."

Just then, Poppy had one of her excellent ideas. "You would be much safer," she said, "if you lived under the hedgerow."

And they did. All day in the meadow, there's munching, mooing and mumbling. All night in the hedgerow, there's nibbling, digging and wiggling. And everyone is happy.

Katy
and the
Butterfly

As Katy Kitten lay dozing happily in the sun, something tickled her nose. It was a butterfly! She tapped at it with her soft paw and it fluttered away. Katy sprang after the butterfly, missed it and landed with a howl in a bed of thistles. "I'll catch that butterfly!" she said, crossly.

Katy chased the butterfly towards the stream, where it settled on the branch of a tree. She climbed after it, high into the tree but, every time she came near, the butterfly simply flew away – and by now, she was stuck! Nervously, she looked down at the stream swirling below her. Then the butterfly fluttered past her nose. Without thinking, Katy swiped at it with her paw. But she lost her balance and went tumbling down through the tree, landing with a great SPLASH! in the water below. Luckily she caught hold of an overhanging branch and clambered out.

Katy arrived home, cold and wet. As she dozed, exhausted, in front of the fire, she felt something tugging at her whiskers. She opened one eye and saw a little mouse.

"Oh no, I've done enough chasing for one day, thank you!" said Katy.

Bella Bunny's Bonnet

In pretty Primrose Wood, there was great excitement. It was the Spring Parade and a prize was being given for the best bonnet.

"I bet I'll win," said Bella, who was a very vain bunny. "What can I use for my hat?" she wondered. She gathered some pretty Spring flowers, then called her friend, Binky the pigeon, for help. The friends worked hard, weaving daffodils and bluebells into a beautiful display.

At last, all the animals were wearing their bonnets, and the parade began. "Mine is the prettiest," giggled Bella, "it's good enough to eat!"

Gordy the goat agreed. Trotting behind Bella, he nibbled her bonnet, until he had gobbled up nearly all the flowers! Then, Holly the horse gave a loud neigh. "The winner of this year's parade is Felicity the fox!" she said.

Everyone cheered – except Bella. "But mine is the best – look!" and whisked off her hat. "Oh no! My hat!" she cried, looking at a clump of twigs!

"But you have won something," sniggered Holly. "The prize for the funniest hat!"

Brave
Billy Bunny

At the edge of Frog Pond Wood, there lived a little bunny called Billy, his brother Bobby and lots of bunny friends. The one thing Billy really, really hated was getting wet! One sunny day, the other bunnies and Bobby hopped off to the stream, to play. "Come on, Billy!" they called.

"No way!" cried Billy. "I hate the water!" What Billy loved doing most of all was running. So, while the other bunnies played at the stream, Billy ran through the wood, leaping logs and weaving round the trees – he was very fast! Suddenly, Bouncer Bunny came rushing back from the stream.

"Come quickly!" he panted. "Bobby's fallen in the stream and is being washed away!" Billy rushed off towards the stream where he found his little brother, Bobby, splashing away in the rushing water. Then, Billy really ran! He got ahead of Bobby and jumped into the water, caught his brother and, coughing and spluttering, dragged poor Bobby to the side.

"Billy!" cried the others. "You're a hero!"

"A wet hero!" said Billy, grinning. "Getting wet wasn't so bad after all. I'm going for another swim!"

One Snowy Day

O ne snowy day, Old Bear poked his nose out of his den, and saw the deep snow that had fallen while he slept. "I'll take a stroll in the woods," he said. Off he went, his great paws padding along, as big white snowflakes tickled his nose. How he loved the snow! He walked far into the woods, deep in thought, and quite forgot to look where he was going.

After a while, Old Bear stopped and looked around. To his dismay, he realised he was quite lost. Then he spied the trail of pawprints behind him. "Ho, ho!" he chuckled. "I'm not lost! I can follow my pawprints home!" And, thinking what a clever old bear he was, he carried on walking, until at last he began to feel tired.

"I'll just take a rest," he said to himself. He closed his eyes, and soon fell fast asleep. Meanwhile, the snow kept on falling, and by the time Old Bear woke up his trail of pawprints had disappeared!

"I'll never find my way home!" he groaned. Then, he noticed an old tree stump nearby. "That looks familiar. And so does that fallen log over there. If I'm not mistaken, I've walked in a big circle, and ended up at home!" he chuckled, turning towards his den. "What a clever old bear I am, after all!"

It's Not Fair!

"I want to swim with the ducklings," said Kitten to Mother Cat, as they walked past the pond.

"You can't," Mother Cat told her. "Your fur isn't waterproof."

"It's not fair!" shouted Kitten. "Kittens don't have any fun!"

"I want to roll in the mud with the piglets," said Kitten, when they walked past the pigsty.

"You can't," Mother Cat told her. "Your long fur will get knotted and matted with mud."

"It's not fair!" shouted Kitten. "Kittens don't have any fun!"

"I want to fly with the baby birds," said Kitten to Mother Cat, as she tried to climb where baby birds were learning to fly.

"You can't," Mother Cat told her. "You have fur, not feathers and you haven't got wings. Kittens aren't meant to fly."

"It's not fair!" shouted Kitten. "Kittens don't have any fun!"

Later, Kitten curled up on a rug by the kitchen fire, with a big saucer of milk. Out of the corner of her eye, kitten saw a movement by the kitchen door.

"I want to sleep by the fire," said Duckling, standing at the door.

Then she heard Piglet say "And I want to lie on a rug," as she trotted past the door.

"And I want to drink a saucer of milk," said a Baby Bird as he flew past.

"It's not fair!" shouted Duckling, Piglet and Baby Bird as Mother Cat shooed them away.

"Oh yes, it is!" mewed Kitten, smiling!

Super Snakes

One morning, Seymour Snake's dad, Seymour Senior, said, "I have a surprise, son! Your cousin Sadie is coming to visit!"

"SSSensational!" said Seymour. "We'll have so much fun playing together, just like we did when we were little!"

"Sadie may have changed a bit since you last saw her," said Seymour Senior. "She's been going to Madame Sylvia's Snake School."

Later that day, Seymour slithered down the path to greet his cousin. "Sadie!" cried Seymour. "It's so good to see you! Come and meet my friends!" Seymour said eagerly. "You can play games with us, and… "

"Oh, I can't play games," Sadie interrupted. "Madame Sylvia always says, 'A well-behaved snake may slither and glide and wriggle and slide, but we DON'T swing or sway, or climb or play!'"

"You don't climb trees and swing from branches?" asked Seymour.

"Certainly not!" said Sadie.

"Well, will you come and meet my friends?" Seymour asked hopefully.

"Oh course," said Sadie. "It would be rude not to!"

"HEY, SEYMOUR!" shouted Maxine Monkey. "Come and play with us!"

"Sure!" said Seymour. "By the way, this is my cousin Sadie."

"HI, SADIE!" shouted Mickey. Maxine and Mickey always shouted! "You can come and play, too."

"No, thank you," said Sadie. "I'll just watch. I don't swing or sway, or climb or play."

So Sadie watched as Seymour climbed a tree, hooked his tail tightly round a branch, and hung down with his mouth wide open.

Mickey and Maxine threw coconuts for him to catch.

"It really is fun, Sadie," Seymour called to his cousin. "Are you sure you don't want to try?"

"It looks good," Sadie admitted, "but no. Thank you anyway."

The game had just finished when Penelope Parrot arrived. Seymour introduced her to Sadie, then Penelope asked if they would help her practise her stunt flying.

"Sure, Penelope!" said Seymour and wound himself round the branch to make two loops. With a whooosh Penelope zoomed through the loops.

Seymour spent hours hanging and swinging and climbing – he even climbed to the very top of a tree to talk to Jeremy Giraffe. Each time, Seymour invited Sadie to join him. And each time, Sadie looked more tempted – but she always said the same thing: "I mustn't swing or sway, or climb or play."

Later, Seymour spoke to his dad. "I'm sure Sadie wants to play with me and my friends," he said. "But she insists on only watching. How can I get her to join in?"

"The only way," said Seymour Senior, "is to get Sadie to see for herself how much fun she could be having."

Suddenly, Seymour had an idea.

"Thanks, Dad," he said. "That's just what I'll do!"

The next morning, Sadie was showing Seymour how gracefully she could glide, when suddenly there was a cry of "OH, NO!" Ellen, Emma and Eric Elephant were staring up into a tree. They looked very upset.

"What's wrong?" Sadie asked.

"We were playing Fling the Melon," said Ellen, "and it got stuck in the tree. Our trunks aren't long enough to reach it!"

"Oh, dear," said Sadie. "I'm sure Seymour will be happy to climb up and get it back for you. Won't you, Seymour? Seymour, where are you?"

Seymour had disappeared!

"Can't you help us, Sadie?" asked Emma.

"I'm sorry," said Sadie, "but I DON'T swing or sway…"

"…or climb or play," Emma finished. "We know about Madame Sylvia's rules. But didn't she also teach you that it's important to help others?" she asked.

"Well," said Sadie, "she did say that we must never pass up a chance to do a good deed."

"And this would be a good deed!" said Eric. "We would be so grateful!"

"I'll do it!" Sadie decided.

Up Sadie went, winding round the trunk, and weaving her way up into the branches, until she reached the melon at the very top.

"Here it comes!" she shouted to the elephants, giving the melon a shove with her nose. It fell straight down into Ellen's waiting trunk. Then, with a quick wriggle, Sadie coiled herself round the branch and hung upside down above the elephants.

"This is SSSTUPENDOUS!" Sadie shouted. "I haven't had so much fun in years!" She swung herself over to another tree, "WHEEEEEEEE!" she cried.

"I knew you'd enjoy this," said Seymour, slithering out from his hiding place. "You just had to try!"

"Come up, Seymour!" Sadie called. "Let's swing and sway together."

"Here I come, Sadie," said Seymour, whizzing up the tree. "But what will you tell Madame Sylvia when you go back to school?"

"I'll tell her," said Sadie, "that we MUST climb and play, and swing and sway – ALL DAY!"

To which they all added a loud, "Hip-hip-HOORAY!"

Home Sweet Home

Old MacDonald always worked hard, but lately he had been extra busy in his workshop. One bright, sunny morning, he was ready to show everyone what he had been making.

"Here you are, ladies!" he cried. "A new henhouse for you – and Henry the cockerel, of course. I didn't like to think of you shivering in your drafty old home.

Jenny and the other hens hurried to look, clucking with curiosity. Henry flapped up to the roof to see if it was a comfortable place for crowing.

"Cock-a-doodle-not-bad-at-all," he crowed, as Jenny, Henrietta, Mary and Victoria hopped in to look at their new home.

For two days the hens were happy in their new house. But the ducks, being rather jealous, squawked and squabbled and sulked in a rather obvious way!

On the third day, Jenny the hen said what the other hens had been thinking. "There was something to be said for the cracks in our old home," she clucked. "We could even keep an eye on those daft ducks without ever having to venture outside."

Henry crowed his agreement, and then all the other hens joined in with their opinions...

"Yes," agreed Henrietta. "And our old perches were much more comfortable, too."

"And," clucked Mary, "this place smells funny! I suppose it's the paint, but I'm not sure I'd want to bring up chicks in here."

Soon the hens and Henry decided they wanted to move back to their old home.

"I could cock-a-doodle-doo right over the pigsty from there," said Henry. "And I used to like chatting to Percy first thing in the morning."

That evening, when Mrs MacDonald came out to feed the hens, Old MacDonald came, too. "Doesn't that look better?" he said, proudly patting the henhouse roof.

"It's a bit too near the flower garden for my liking," said his wife, looking at Henry, who was very fond of eating all her marigolds!

The hens knew that Old MacDonald was proud of the new henhouse. They couldn't bear to hurt his feelings by returning to their old home, so they would just have to make do with this one.

A few days later, it was Milly the farm cat – who wasn't the best of friends with any of the feathered folk on the farm – who solved the problem.

While the hens and Henry were in the barn, Milly crept into the brand new henhouse.

It was just the cosy place she needed. "Mmm, this is purr-fect," she said.

So, very quietly Old MacDonald had a word with Henry and the hens. "Sorry," he said, "but Milly had her kittens in your new home. We won't be able to disturb her for a few weeks. Could you..."

Before he could finish, they were scuttling through the door of their dear old home. It's amazing how helpful they can be sometimes!

Water Hunt

In the higgledy-piggledy, messy alley it was a very hot day. Harvey and his gang were melting!

"I need a slurpy, slippy ice lolly," sighed Ruffles.

"I need a cool pool to roll in," squeaked Puddles. Those hot dogs just didn't know what to do!

"It's even too hot to sleep," complained Bonnie. "I'm the hottest dog in the whole world!"

"I bet I'm hotter than you!" snorted Ruffles.

"I haven't been this hot," said Mac, "since I was in the desert when…"

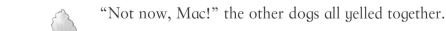

"Not now, Mac!" the other dogs all yelled together.

"Stop!" cried Harvey. "It's much too hot to argue! Listen, I know what we'll do… let's play a game. Let's have a water hunt."

"Can I hunt, too?" yelped Puddles, hopping from one hot paw to the other.

"Do we have to move, Harvey?" groaned Patchy. "I don't think I can."

"Come on," said Harvey. "Where can we find some water?"

"I'm too hot to think," wailed Bonnie.

"We're too hot to do anything," said Patchy.

"Except eat yummy, cold ice cream," replied Ruffles, with a grin.

"I know," cried Mac suddenly. "Let's go to the seaside! We could play in the sand and splish and splash in the water."

"Good thinking, Mac," smiled Harvey. "But it's too far for us to go on a day like today. Can you think of something else?"

"I've got a really good idea – diggin'!" grinned Ruffles.

"Digging?" cried the others. "Dig for water in this heat?"

"No," said Ruffles excitedly. "Dig for bones. The dirt will be really damp and cool and we could roll around in it and…"

"No way, Ruffles," said Harvey firmly. "Today is not a digging day."

"Let's all go to the park," suggested Patchy. "We could jump in and out of the paddling pool and play in the fountain."

Poor Puddles looked as though she were going to burst into tears.

"I can't walk far, Harvey," she whispered. "I've only got little legs!"

"Don't worry, Puddles," said Harvey. "We wouldn't go without you."

"Oh, there must be some water somewhere!" Patchy puffed and panted.

"If I don't find water soon, I'm going to melt into a big, hairy puddle!" groaned Ruffles.

"Haven't you got any ideas at all, Harvey?" asked Mac.

But even Harvey was too hot to think, and Bonnie had given up and had gone to sleep in her dustbin!

Those poor hot dogs – what on earth could they do?

Meanwhile, the sizzling Alley Cats were searching, too. But they weren't on a water hunt. Oh no! They were on a mouse hunt – Archie had lost his favourite toy mouse!

"I WANT IT BACK!" wailed Archie, looking under a box.

"Well, it's not in here!" called Bertie from the top of a flower pot.

"Phew!" groaned Hattie. "It's too hot for hunting, Archie. Why don't we have a cat nap instead?"

"Cat nap time!" said Lucy.

So the Alley Cats snuggled down for an afternoon nap – or did they?

Lenny and Lulu – the two little kittens – weren't quite ready for a nap just yet!

"Naps are for babies," whispered Lenny to his sister. "Come on, Lulu, follow me."

"Yippee!" giggled Lulu, "an adventure."

The kittens clambered and climbed over the pots and pans and headed towards a hole in the fence.

"Hey, Lulu!" cried Lenny. "I bet we'll find Archie's mouse through here."

So, carefully and quietly, the kittens squeezed themselves through the tiny gap... Suddenly, a strange, stripy monster jumped up in front of them!

"AAAAAGH!" screamed Lulu. "What is it?"

Swooping and swaying through the spikey grass, the monster wiggled and wiggled towards them. Then it lifted up its head and gave a loud, angry "HISSSSS!"

"Oh no! It's a snake!" yelled Lenny. "Let's scarper."

Running as fast as they could, the kittens fled to a tree and scampered up into its branches!

"We'll be safe up here," gasped Lenny.

But Lenny was wrong!

The sinister snake hissed louder and louder and slithered up the tree after them. Lenny and Lulu quivered and quaked.

"HELP!" they wailed. As the snake swayed about in front of the kittens, the poor little pussies began to cry.

With one, last enormous "HISSSSSSS!", the swinging snake leapt towards them – and got stuck in a branch!

Suddenly a great big spurt of water gushed from the snake's mouth, shot over the fence and into the alley below – SPLOOOSH!

Those silly scallywags. It wasn't a snake at all. It was a hosepipe and the cool refreshing water woke up Harvey and the gang – they couldn't believe their eyes!

"It's rainy and sunny at the same time," laughed Harvey.

He looked up and saw Lenny and Lulu peeping shyly over the fence.

"You clever cats," he called up to them.

"Three cheers for Lenny and Lulu!" cried the Alley Dogs. "HIP! HIP! HOORAY!"

And so, two cool cats had made five hot dogs very happy!

Little Bunny
and the
Bully

Down in Cowslip Meadow lived lots and lots of bunnies. They were all friends and played together happily all day long – all except for one. Big Bunny was a bully! He didn't like the other bunnies having fun and was always teasing and scaring them! He'd hide behind bushes and jump out on them and pull the girls' ears and tweak their tails!

Big Bunny didn't have any friends or anyone to play with, because he was always so mean. But he didn't care!

"Who needs friends, anyway?" he said. "Not me!" And off he hopped, down to the stream. But one of the bunnies felt sorry for Big Bunny.

"Everyone should have a friend," thought Little Bunny, as he hopped after the rabbit. "Hey, Big Bunny," he called. "Would you like to share my carrot cake and be my friend?"

"No!" snarled the naughty bully. "I don't want to share. I want it all!"

And with one big bunny bounce, he grabbed the yummy cake and knocked Little Bunny into the water

– SPLOOSH! "I don't like sharing!" cried Big Bunny, hopping away. "And I don't want you to be my friend!"

Little Bunny shook himself dry and hopped back towards the meadow. "I'm going home," he muttered to himself. "Big Bunny is such a bully."

Suddenly, he heard a noise. It sounded like someone crying. "I wonder what that is?" thought Little Bunny. He hopped towards the edge of a steep bank and peeped over. There, at the very bottom, sat Big Bunny!

"Please help me, Little Bunny!" he called, weakly. "I've hurt my paw and I can't climb up!" Little Bunny bounced into action!

"Don't worry, I'll get some help!" he called to Big Bunny and raced off home, as fast as he could.

And, even though Big Bunny had always been so mean to the other rabbits of Cowslip Meadow, when Little Bunny cried, "Big Bunny is hurt," they all rushed to help.

Little Bunny's daddy climbed down the bank and rescued the scared, injured rabbit.

"I'm sorry for being so nasty to you," cried Big Bunny, as he gave Little Bunny a big hug. "Thank you for saving me!"

"Well, that's what friends are for!" chuckled Little Bunny and everyone cheered!

Lazy Teddy

There was nothing Lazy Teddy liked more than to be tucked up snug and warm in Joshua's bed.

Every morning the alarm clock would ring and Joshua would leap out of bed and fling open the curtains. "I love mornings!" he'd say, stretching his arms up high as the sun poured in through the window.

"You're crazy!" Teddy would mutter, and he'd burrow down beneath the quilt to the bottom of the bed, where he'd spend the rest of the morning snoozing happily.

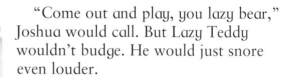

"Come out and play, you lazy bear," Joshua would call. But Lazy Teddy wouldn't budge. He would just snore even louder.

Joshua wished that Teddy would be more lively, like his other friends' bears. He loved having adventures, but they would be better if Teddy would share them with him.

One evening, Joshua decided to have a talk with Teddy before they went to bed. He told him about the fishing trip he'd been on that day with his friends and their teddy bears.

"It was lots of fun, Teddy. I wish you'd been there. It really is time you stopped being such a lazybones. Tomorrow is my birthday, and I'm having a party. There will be lots of games, and presents and ice cream. Please promise you'll come?"

"It does sound like fun," said Teddy. "Okay, I promise. I'll get up just this once."

The next morning, Joshua was up bright and early. "Yippee, it's my birthday today!" he yelled, dancing around the room. He pulled the covers off his bed. "Come on, Teddy, time to get up!"

"Just five more minutes!" groaned Teddy, and he rolled over and fell straight back to sleep. When Joshua came back up to his room after breakfast, Teddy still wasn't up.

Well, by now Joshua was getting quite cross with Teddy. He reached over and poked him in the tummy. Teddy opened one eye and growled. "Wake up, Teddy! You promised, remember?" said Joshua.

Teddy yawned. "Oh, if I must!" he said, and muttering and grumbling he climbed out of bed. He washed his face and paws, brushed his teeth and put on his best red waistcoat.

"There, I'm ready!" he said.

"Good," said Joshua. "About time too!"

Just then the doorbell rang, and Joshua ran to answer it. "I'll come and fetch you in a minute," he said to Teddy. But when he returned there was no sign of Teddy, just a gentle snoring down the bottom of the bed.

Joshua was so cross and upset with Lazy Teddy, that he decided to leave him right where he was.

"He'll just have to miss the party!" he said. Deep down though, he was hurt that Teddy wouldn't keep his promise.

Joshua enjoyed his party, although he wished that Teddy had been there. That night, when he got into bed, he cried quietly into his pillow.

Teddy lay awake in the dark, listening. He knew Joshua was crying because he had let him down, and he felt very ashamed.

"I'm sorry!" whispered Lazy Teddy, and he snuggled up to Joshua and stroked him with a paw until he fell asleep.

The next morning when the alarm clock rang, Joshua leapt out of bed, as usual. But what was this? Teddy had leapt out of bed too, and was stretching his paws up high. Joshua looked at him in amazement.

"What are we doing today, then?" asked Teddy.

"G...g...going for a picnic," stammered Joshua, in surprise. "Are you coming?"

"Of course," said Teddy. And from that day on, Teddy was up bright and early every day, ready to enjoy another day of fun and adventures with Joshua, and Teddy never let him down again.

The Chicklings

Duck and Hen both laid some eggs. They were very proud mothers. They sat for days on their nests, waiting for their eggs to hatch.

"Duck," said Hen, "let us put the eggs side by side, and see whose eggs are the most beautiful."

"If you like," said Duck, "but I already know mine are."

"Ha!" said Hen. "Wait until you have seen mine!"

Duck and Hen each carried their eggs, one by one, to a spot where there was soft hay on the ground. They both looked at how smooth the eggs were. Hen picked up an egg too. Then they both looked at the shape of the egg. Then they put back those two eggs and picked up two others.

By the time the last one was picked up and put back, the eggs were all mixed up together! As Hen was fatter than Duck, she picked out the largest eggs and took them back to her nest, and duck took the others back to hers. Then they sat on them until they hatched.

One day, Duck and Hen met with their babies. Duck was teaching her ducklings how to be ducklings.

"Walk behind me, in a line!" she told them. "We are going to have swimming lessons." But the ducklings just couldn't walk in single file. They ran circles around Duck. They ran over her and under her, until Duck became quite dizzy watching them. At the pond, the ducklings dipped their feet in the water, shook their heads and refused to go in!

Hen was teaching her chicks how to be chicks. She taught them to scratch and hop to make the worms pop up out of the ground. But the chicks fell on their faces instead, and followed her everywhere in a line.

Duck and Hen knew by now that they had each taken the wrong eggs. The ducklings were chicks, and the chicks were ducklings.

"Never mind," said Hen. "Let's just call them Chicklings, and we will always be right."

And the duck chicklings played happily in the dog's bowl... and the chick chicklings played on the dog!

I Love My Puppy

I love my puppy because he wags his tail and comes to meet me. He barks and jumps in the air when he wants to play, and chases my big bouncy ball. He fetches a stick for me to throw. He scampers beside me when we go for walks in the park.

But I love him most when he is sleepy and we snuggle up close.

I Love My Kitten

I love my kitten because she purrs softly when I stroke her. She pounces on a ball of wool and rolls it between her paws. She runs along the garden wall and leaps over the gate. She washes her face by licking her soft padded paws. She peeps through the cat flap to see if her dinner is ready.

But I love her most of all when she sits with her tail curled all around herself.

I Love My Pony

I love my pony because he neighs hello when I come to visit him. He lets me sponge him and brush his soft shiny mane. He eats a shiny green apple right out of my hand. He's fun to be with when we go for long rides. He jumps at the show and wins a bright red rosette.

But I love him most of all when I talk to him and he nuzzles up close.

I Love My Bunny

I love my bunny because he twitches his nose, and has smooth silky fur. Bunny nibbles a carrot with his bright white teeth. He runs in the garden and his fluffy white tail bobs up and down. He digs a hole in the lawn with his big soft paws. He sits quietly as I stroke his big floppy ears, and his whiskers twitch up and down.

But I love him most when he dozes off to sleep sitting on my lap.

Danny Duckling in Trouble

"Just as I thought, Danny's missing again. We'd better go and look for him!" quacked Mummy Duck, crossly. It was the third time that week Danny Duckling had got lost, and this time he was in trouble...

Earlier that day, Danny had been following the family, paddling through the reeds when his foot caught in something beneath the water.

"Bother!" he quacked. His foot was tangled in an old fishing net held fast in the mud. "Help!" he cried, but the others were too far away to hear. The more Danny struggled, the tighter the net gripped his foot.

Luckily, Freya Frog heard his cries and dived under the water to try and free him, but it was no use. So Freya fetched Wally Water Rat.

In no time at all, Wally's sharp teeth nibbled through the net, and Danny bobbed back to the surface just as his mummy appeared.

"Thank goodness you're safe," said Mummy. "But from now on swim at the front of the line." And that is just what Danny did.

Jimbo
Comes
Home

Jimbo the circus elephant was snoring away in his cage one night when he heard a strange noise. At first he thought it was part of his dream. In his dream he was walking across a hot, dusty plain while in the distance there was the sound of thunder.

All at once Jimbo was wide awake. He realised that he was in his cage after all and that what he thought was the sound of thunder was the noise of his cage on the move. Now this worried him, because the circus never moved at night. He rose to his feet and looked around.

Zipper's Circus

He could see men pulling on the tow bar at the front of the cage. These were strangers – it certainly wasn't Carlos his trainer! Jimbo started to bellow, "Help! Stop thief!" But it was too late. His cage was already rumbling out of the circus ground and down the road.

Eventually, the cage passed through a gate marked "Zipper's Circus" and Jimbo knew what had happened. He had been stolen by the Zipper family, his own circus family's greatest rivals! Jimbo was furious. How had the thieves got away with it? Surely someone at Ronaldo's Circus must have heard the noise when they stole him? But Jimbo waited in vain to be rescued.

The next morning, the thieves opened up Jimbo's cage and tried to coax him out, but he stayed put. In the end, after much struggling, they managed to pull him out. Once he was out of his cage, he took the biggest drink of water he could from a bucket and soaked his new keeper!

He refused to cooperate, kicked over his food, and when he appeared in the circus that night he made sure he got all the tricks wrong.

"Don't worry," said Mr Zipper to Jimbo's new trainer, "he'll just take a little while to settle down. Soon he'll forget that he was once part of Ronaldo's Circus." But Jimbo didn't forget for, as you know, an elephant never forgets.

One night, a mouse passed by his cage. "Hello," called Jimbo mournfully, for by now he was feeling very lonely, and no one had cleaned out his cage for days.

"Hello!" said the mouse. "You don't seem to be very happy. What's the matter?"

Jimbo explained how he had been stolen and wanted to escape back to his own circus.

The mouse listened and then said, "I will try to help." So saying, he scampered off and soon he came back with a big bunch of keys. Jimbo was astonished.

"Easy!" said the mouse. "The keeper was asleep, so I helped myself."

Jimbo took the keys in his trunk and unlocked the door to the cage.

He was free! "Thank you!" he called to the mouse, who was already scurrying away.

Jimbo's first thought was to get back to his own circus as fast as possible. However, he wanted to teach those thieves a lesson. He could hear them snoring in their caravan. He tiptoed up, as quietly as an elephant can tiptoe, and slid into the horse's harness at the front.

"Hey, what do you think you're doing?" neighed one of the horses, but Jimbo was already hauling the robbers' caravan through the gate and down the road.

So gently did he pull the caravan that the thieves never once woke up.

Eventually, they reached Ronaldo's Circus. Mr Ronaldo was dumbstruck to see Jimbo pulling a caravan just like a horse! Mr Ronaldo walked over to the caravan and was astonished to see the robbers still fast asleep.

He raced to the telephone and called the police, and it wasn't until they heard the police siren that the robbers woke up. By then it was too late. As they emerged from the caravan scratching and shaking their heads they were arrested on the spot and taken off to jail.

"There are quite a few questions we would like to ask Mr Zipper regarding the theft of some other circus animals, too," said one of the police officers.

Mr Ronaldo, and Jimbo's keeper Carlos, were both delighted to see

Jimbo back home again. And Jimbo was just as delighted to be back home. Then Mr Ronaldo and Carlos started whispering to each other and began walking away looking secretive. "We'll be back soon, we promise," they said to Jimbo. When they returned, they were pushing Jimbo's old cage. It had been freshly painted, there was clean, sweet-smelling straw inside, but best of all there was no lock on the door! "Now you can come and go as you please," said Carlos.

And Jimbo trumpeted long and loud with his trunk held high, which Carlos knew was his way of saying, "THANK YOU!"

Teddy Bear Tears

As a little fairy called Mavis flew past the rubbish dump, she heard a sound coming from the other side of a very smelly pile of rubbish. "Oh dear. Those sound like teddy bear tears," she said to herself, and flew down to take a look. She found a very old, very sad teddy.

Teddy told Mavis how his owner, Matilda, was told to clean out her room. "She's terribly messy, but she's sweet and kind," Teddy sniffed. "She threw me out with an old blanket – she didn't realise I was inside, having a sleep. Then some men in a big, dirty truck emptied me out of the dustbin and brought me here. But I want to go home!"

"I'll help you," said Mavis, "but I need two teddy bear tears." So she scooped two big tears into a jar from Teddy's cheeks. "Now wait here, I promise I'll be back soon." And with that, she disappeared!

Mavis flew back and forth, until she heard the sound of sobbing coming from an open window. She flew down and peered inside. A little girl was lying on the bed, with her mummy sitting beside her.

"I want my teddy!" she cried.

"Try to sleep now," said Mummy, "and we'll look for Teddy in the morning."

Mavis watched until poor Matilda fell fast asleep. Then Mavis flew down, took out the little jar, and rubbed Teddy's tears onto Matilda's sleeping eyes. With a fizzle of magic stars, Matilda started to dream. She could see a rubbish dump... her blanket, and there, wrapped inside it was her teddy, with a big tear running down his cheek!

The next morning, Matilda remembered her dream at once. She ran to the kitchen and told Mummy all about it. "We have to go to the rubbish dump! We have to save Teddy!" said Matilda.

Mummy tried to explain that it was just a dream, but Matilda wouldn't listen, she was sure she was right. So in the end they set off to take a look.

Mavis hovered in the air above Teddy and waved her wand in a bright flash. Matilda spotted him at once.

"There he is!" she shouted, crying with relief.

Soon Teddy and Matilda were reunited... and from then on, Matilda's room was the tidiest room you have ever seen.

Gym Giraffe

Jeremy Giraffe loved going out with his dad to gather the juicy green leaves for their dinner.

"This is where the most delicious leaves are," said Dad, reaching w-a-a-a-y up to a very high branch. "Remember the tallest trees have the tastiest leaves, and the tiny top leaves are the tenderest!"

One morning, Jeremy decided it was time to gather leaves on his own. "The tallest trees have the tastiest leaves," he whispered to himself, "and the tiny top leaves are the tenderest."

Jeremy stopped at a very tall tree and looked up. There at the top were some tiny, tender, tasty-looking leaves. Str - e - e - e - etching his neck just as he had seen his dad do, Jeremy reached as high as he could. It wasn't very high! "Oh, no," he thought. "How will I reach the tiny, tasty top leaves if my neck won't stretch?"

So Jeremy went back home with his neck hanging down in despair.

"Why, Jeremy, what's wrong?" asked his mum. When Jeremy told her, she gave his neck a nuzzle. "Your neck's still growing," she assured him. "Eat your greens and get lots of sleep, and you'll soon be able to reach the tastiest, tenderest leaves on the tallest trees in the jungle!"

That afternoon, Jeremy went out to try again. Portia Parrot saw Jeremy struggling to reach the top of the tree. Thinking that she would be helpful, she swooped down and plucked a few of the tenderest leaves for him.

When Portia gave Jeremy the leaves, his spots went pale with shame and embarrassment.

"Portia, I should be able to get those myself," he wailed. "Why won't my neck stretch?"

"Oh, Jeremy," said Portia, "your neck is just fine! Keep eating your greens and getting lots of sleep, and it will grow!"

"But I can't wait," Jeremy insisted. "Isn't there anything I can do to stretch my neck now?"

"Perhaps there is," said Portia, thoughtfully. "Follow me!"

Portia led Jeremy through the jungle to a clearing. Jeremy's eyes widened with wonder at what he saw. There was so much going on! Seymour Snake was wrapping himself round a fallen tree trunk. "Hello, Jeremy," he hissed. "Jusssssst doing my sssssslithering exercisesssss!"

Emma, Ellen and Eric Elephant were hoisting logs. "Hi, Jeremy," they called. "This is our trunk-strengthening workout!"

In the river, Claudia Crocodile was breaking thick branches in half. "Just limbering up my jaw muscles," she snapped.

Leonard Lion was taking his cubs, Louis and Lisa, through their pouncing paces. "Welcome to the Jungle Gym!" he called.

Then, Grandpa Gorilla and Leonard Lion came to greet Jeremy.

"What can we do for you?" they asked.

"Can you help me stretch my neck?" asked Jeremy. "I want to be able to reach the tasty, tiny, tender leaves."

"You're still growing," said Leonard Lion. "You just have to eat your greens and get lots of sleep."

Jeremy's face fell, until Grandpa Gorilla said, "But we will help things along with some special neck-stretching exercises. Come with us!"

Grandpa got Jeremy started on his exercises right away.

"S-t-r-e-t-c-h to the left! S-t-r-e-t-c-h to the right!" Grandpa Gorilla shouted.

"Then we will do chin lifts next," said Leonard Lion.

Jeremy s-t-r-e-e-e-t-c-h-e-d his neck to reach the branch.

"Come on, you can do it!" Portia said, cheering him on.

Grandpa Gorilla told Jeremy to lie down. Then he called Seymour Snake. "Start slithering!" he said.

"Aaakk!" gasped Jeremy, as Seymour wrapped himself round his neck.

"Not so tight," said Grandpa.

"That's better!" said Jeremy, as Seymour slithered along, pu-u-u-l-l-ing his neck muscles. All the exercise made Jeremy hungry.

At supper, he had three BIG helpings of greens. He was tired, too, so he went to bed early and slept soundly.

Jeremy loved the Jungle Gym and couldn't wait to go back. After his workout each day, Jeremy ate a good supper.

"Exercising makes me sooo hungry… " he said, "… and soooo tired," he yawned, as he fell asleep.

The next time Jeremy and his dad went out leaf-gathering, Jeremy spotted some sweet-looking leaves at the top of a tall tree.

"I'm going to get those," he said.

"They're so high up!" said Dad.

Jeremy didn't hear him. He was too busy stretching... and stretching... and stretching... until he stretched right up to the very top branch!

"I've done it, Dad!" he cried happily. "The exercises worked!"

"I don't think it matters," said his mum. "What matters is that you have a fine, strong, long neck that any giraffe would be proud of!"

"And I am!" said Jeremy, taking another mouthful of tasty, tender leaves. He chewed the leaves extra thoroughly – because he knew they had a very long way to go!

The Naughty Kitten

Ginger was a naughty little kitten. He didn't always mean to be naughty, but somehow things just turned out that way.

"You really should be more careful," warned Mummy. But Ginger was too busy getting into trouble to listen.

One day, Ginger was in a particularly playful mood. First, he tried to play tag with his smallest sister – and chased her right up an old apple tree. It took Daddy all morning to get her down.

Then, Ginger dropped cream all over the dog's tail. The dog whirled round and round as he tried to lick it off. He got so dizzy that he fell right over. That really made Ginger laugh until his sides hurt.

Next, Ginger thought it would be fun to play hide-and-seek with the mice – and they were so frightened that they refused to come out of their hole for the rest of the day.

Then, Ginger crept up behind the rabbit and shouted, "HI!" The poor rabbit was so surprised that he fell into his breakfast.

For his next trick, Ginger knocked over a wheelbarrow full of apples while he was trying to fly like a bird, and then he laughed when the apples knocked his little brother flying into the air. One of the apples splashed into the garden pond, so Ginger decided to go apple bobbing. He laughed at the goldfish as they hurried to get out of his way.

Ginger laughed so much that, WHO-OO-AH! he began to lose his balance. He stopped laughing as he tried to stop himself falling into the pond. But, SPLASH! it was no good – he fell right in.

"Help! I can't swim," wailed Ginger, splashing wildly around. But he needn't have worried, the water only reached up to his knees.

"Yuck!" he moaned, squirting out a mouthful of water.

"Ha, ha, ha!" laughed the other kittens, who had come to see what the noise was about. And the dog and the rabbit soon joined in.

"You really should be more careful," said Mummy, trying not to smile.

"It's not funny," said Ginger. He gave the other animals a hard glare as Daddy pulled him out of the pond. But then he caught sight of his reflection in the water. He did look very funny. Soon he was laughing as loudly as the others.

After that, Ginger tried hard not to be quite so naughty. And do you know what? He even succeeded... some of the time!

Little Lost Lenny

One grey day, Lenny the kitten was happily chasing his twin sister, Lulu, around the higgledy-piggledy, messy alley. They were having great fun, leaping over boxes and jumping through tyres.

Hattie, their mummy, looked up at the big, dark clouds. "I think we had better tidy up before it rains," she said. "Come on, everyone, let's put everything away."

So Uncle Bertie and Cousin Archie moved the boxes.

Auntie Lucy helped Hattie tidy away the blankets. Even little Lulu helped by clearing away her toys – she didn't want the rain to make them squelchy and soggy!

Everyone was busy helping... or were they?

That little mischief-maker, Lenny, was planning something naughty! He hid behind Lulu's dustbin, then leapt out and snatched her teddy.

With a giggle, he ran off down the alley. Lulu gave a long wail. Teddy was her favourite toy.

"Mummy!" she yelled. "Lenny's got my teddy!"

Lenny stopped at the bottom of the alley and called to his sister.

"If you want Teddy," he said, "come and get him."

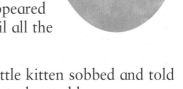

Lulu raced down the alley.

Lenny giggled and tossed the teddy high into the sky. He went straight over his sister's head and disappeared behind a large fence! Lulu stood and wailed until all the other cats came charging down the alley.

"Whatever's the matter?" cried Hattie. The little kitten sobbed and told her mummy what her naughty brother had done to her teddy.

Everyone looked at Lenny.

"Lenny, you really are a naughty pussy!" said his mother, crossly. "You know you're not supposed to come down to this part of the alley."

Bertie scooped up Lulu. "Don't worry," he said, kindly. "Archie and I will find Teddy for you later." Lenny stood still, bit his lip and trembled.

"Why do you have to get into so much trouble?" asked Hattie. "And why can't you be more helpful like your sister?" And off she stomped, back towards her dustbin.

"Sorry, Mummy," whispered Lenny.

A big, fat tear trickled down his cheek.

"It's not fair," he thought. "I didn't mean to lose silly old Teddy!"

Lenny gave a sniff and wandered over to the gate. He peeped through the rusty iron bars. Mummy had said that they must never, ever go through this gate.

"But I don't know why," thought Lenny.

"I do know that Teddy's in there, though," he said, "and I must try and get him back."

So he squeezed himself through the bars…

Lenny found himself standing at the edge of a big building site. There were wooden planks and piles of bricks everywhere – Lenny thought it looked great fun.

"I don't know why Mummy told me to keep away from here," he laughed. "It's like having my very own adventure playground."

The naughty pussy soon forgot about feeling sad as he climbed ladders and walked across gangplanks, high above the ground.

"I'm Lucky Lenny the Pirate!" he laughed. Then he stopped and peered through the rain.

"And there's Teddy!" he cried.

As Lenny grabbed the bear, the plank tipped up. The rain had made it very slippery and... down, down, down he fell – all the way to the bottom of a mucky, muddy hole.

Luckily, cats always land on their feet, so he wasn't hurt, but he'd had a real fright!

Lenny's little claws tried to grip the sides of the hole, but the rain had loosened the soil. It sprinkled down all over his head!

Oh dear, now he really was stuck!

"Mummy! Mummy!" he meowed. "Help! I'm stuck!"

Meanwhile, back in the alley, the cats were sheltering from the rain. Suddenly, Hattie looked round.

"Where's Lenny?" she asked, but no one had seen him for ages.

Hattie ran out into the alley. "Lenny!" she cried through the pouring rain. "Lenny, where are you?" She knew something was wrong.

"Go and get the dogs," she said to Archie. "Ask them to help us find my poor, little Lenny."

Archie quickly returned with Harvey and the gang.

"Don't worry, Hattie," said Harvey. "We'll soon find him."

All the dogs and cats ran out into the pouring rain, meowing and barking Lenny's name. At the bottom of the alley, the Old English Sheepdog, Ruffles, sniffed.

"I can smell him!" he yelped. "He's very near!" He snuffled to the gate.

"Yes, he's in there!" cried Patchy, the dog with a patch over one eye, "I can hear him crying!"

The animals rushed through the gate and quickly found the muddy hole where Lenny was stuck.

"Don't worry!" called Harvey. "We'll soon get you out."

Uncle Bertie found a thick rope. "We can use this," he called.

Ruffles, Harvey and Bertie lowered the rope to Lenny. The tiny kitten clung on tight and was pulled to safety. Lenny gave Teddy back to Lulu. "I didn't mean to make you sad," he said.

"We were all so worried about you!" said Hattie. "There will be no kitty treats for you tonight."

"I'm really sorry, Mummy," sniffed Lenny.

Hattie smiled and gave her naughty, little kitten a big hug and a big kiss. "That's okay," she smiled. "At least you're safe now."

Then, all the Alley Cats went back to the alley for lots of cat-napping!

Milly the Greedy Puppy

Milly the Labrador puppy just loved eating. She wasn't fussy about what she ate, and didn't really mind whom it belonged to.

"You'll get fat," warned Tom, the farm cat. But Milly was too busy chewing a tasty fishbone to take any notice.

One day, Milly sneaked into the kitchen and ate Tom's biscuits. After her own breakfast of fresh sardines and milk, she had a short break before nibbling her way through the horse's oats. Then, after a quick nap, Milly felt quite hungry, so she ate all the tastiest titbits from the pigs' trough. But she made sure she left plenty of room for her lunch!

After a light lunch, Milly couldn't help feeling just a bit hungry – so she knocked over the dustbin and rifled through the kitchen waste. It was full of the yummiest leftovers. Then there was just enough time for another nap before nipping into the milking shed at milking time to lap up the odd bucketful of fresh milk when Farmer Jones wasn't looking.

Dinner was Milly's favourite. It was amazing how fast she could eat a huge bowl of meat and biscuits.

Before going to bed, Milly walked around the yard cleaning up the scraps the hens had left behind. Just as Milly was chewing a particularly tasty bit of bread, she saw Tom the farm cat, out for his evening stroll. If there was one thing Milly liked doing best of all, it was eating Tom's dinner when he wasn't looking.

Milly raced across the yard, around the barn and through the cat flap.

"Woof! Woof!" yelped Milly. She was stuck half-way through the cat flap. Greedy Milly had eaten so much food that her tummy was too big to fit through.

"Ha! Ha!" laughed the farm animals, who thought it served Milly right for eating all their food.

"Oh, dear!" smiled Tom when he came back to see what all the noise was about. He caught hold of Milly's back legs and tried pulling her out. Then he tried pushing her out. But it was no good – she was stuck.

All the farm animals joined in. They pulled and pulled, until, POP! Out flew Milly.

Poor Milly felt so silly that she never ate anyone else's food again – unless they offered, that is!

Kissable Kitten

In a corner of the kitchen, Mummy Cat lay in her basket and purred happily. Curled up asleep near her were four beautiful kittens – a grey kitten called Timmy, a black kitten called Winnie and a stripy kitten called Ginger. And then there was Kissy, the softest, cutest kitten you ever did see!

Timmy had the biggest blue eyes. They spotted everything. When he and Kissy were in the garden, chasing bumble bees, it was Timmy who spied the water sprinkler.

"Watch out, Kissy!" called Timmy. "The sprinkler is on and we'll get wet!"

"Splish, splash, flipperty-flash!" sang Kissy. "I don't care!" And she pushed through the flowers with her little pink nose and shrieked with laughter, as the water sprinkler suddenly covered them both with water.

"Kissy!" spluttered Timmy, shaking water drops from his ears. "Now look what you've done!"

But Kissy just rolled around, laughing. "Oh, Timmy," she giggled. "That was so funny!"

"Goodness me," said Mummy Cat, as her kittens dripped water on to the kitchen floor. "Timmy Kitten! You shouldn't have let Kissy get so wet! Now I shall have to dry you both!"

Kissy wriggled and giggled, as Mummy Cat's rough, pink tongue made her wet fur soft and white again. "Sugar and spice, that feels nice!" she sang. But Timmy wasn't quite so happy. "Ow! Miaow!" he howled, as Mummy Cat's tongue licked him dry.

Kissy loved to explore with Winnie. Winnie had the cutest kitten nose ever and could sniff out all the best yummy food. "Mmm! Smells like jam and cream," said Winnie, her nose and whiskers twitching. Kissy reached up and gently pulled a corner of the tablecloth.

"Mind, Kissy!" said Winnie. "You'll pull everything over!"

"Yum, yum, yum, that cream should be in my tum!" sang Kissy as she pulled the cloth a bit more. Suddenly, the cream jug and jam pot fell to the floor with a crash!

"Oh, Kissy!" shrieked Winnie. "What have you done?"

Jam and cream went everywhere – what a mess! Kissy Kitten could hardly speak for laughing. "Oh, Winnie," she giggled. "That was so funny!"

Mummy Cat threw her paws up in the air in horror when she saw the awful mess they had made.

"Goodness me," she said. "How could you let Kissy get so sticky, Winnie Kitten? Now I shall have to wash you both!"

Kissy giggled, as Mummy Cat licked her clean. "Bibble and bat, I like that!" she sang.

But Winnie wasn't happy at all. "Ow! Miaow!" she cried, as Mummy Cat's rough tongue lapped up the jam.

Kissy loved playing with Ginger because Ginger liked to pretend he was a fierce tiger, hunting wild animals or pouncing on Mummy Cat's twitching tail. Today, they were both hunting a Monster Mouse in the vegetable patch. "There's a dangerous mud puddle over there, Kissy," whispered Ginger. "Whatever you do, don't go in it!"

"Fiddle, fuddle, who cares for a puddle?" sang Kissy as she crawled right through the sticky, squelchy mud. Her beautiful white coat got muddier and muddier. She looked as if she was wearing brown boots!

Ginger hid his eyes. "Oh no! I can't look!" he said. Kissy laughed and laughed. Then, she shook the mud off her dainty paws – all over Ginger!

Mummy Cat howled when she saw her two dirty kittens. "Ginger Kitten! How could you have let Kissy get so muddy?" she cried. "It is going to take me ages to clean you both!"

"Piddle and pud, that feels good!" sang Kissy.

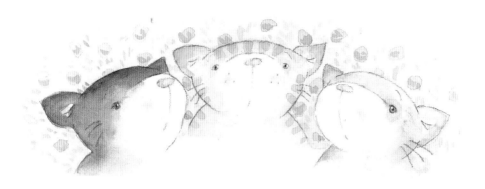

Poor Ginger didn't feel good at all. "Ow! Miaow!" he wailed, as Mummy Cat cleaned up his coat.

Mummy Cat looked at her kittens and shook her head. "I just can't understand it," she said. "You've always been such good kittens!" Timmy, Winnie and Ginger all frowned at Kissy, who was fast asleep, purring in their basket.

"It wasn't us!" they cried. "We told Kissy Kitten to be careful! We don't like being bathed!" cried the kittens. "We don't like getting soaked or covered with sticky stuff or coated with mud!"

Mummy Cat looked into the basket. "Kissy?" she said. Kissy opened a bright, green eye and said, "But Mummy, I just love it when you kiss my nose and wash me every time I get messy!"

"What a funny Kissy Kitten you are!" said Mummy Cat, giving her a big lick. "You can have a kiss any time you want. You don't have to get really messy first!"

"No, we'd prefer it if you didn't!" said Timmy.

"But we forgive you," said Winnie and Ginger.

Kissy promised never to get them messy again. Then, they all cuddled up together in their basket and went fast asleep!

Lost and Alone

Deep in the jungle, Mungo was trying to slip off through the trees. "Mungo, tell me where you're going, please," called Mum.

"I'm just going to play," smiled Mungo, and off he went.

Elephant was enjoying a drink, when Mungo crept up and yelled, "Hi, Elephant! Want to play?" Then he added, "I know a good game called funny faces!" said Mungo. "What do you say?"

"I'm not sure," said Elephant. "I don't know how to play."

"Easy," said Mungo. "All you have to do is pull a funny face, like this… " He took hold of Elephant's trunk, wound it round and slipped the end through, pulling it into a knot. "Wow!" he giggled. "What a funny face you've got!"

"Hey!" gurgled Elephant. "How do I get out of this?" But Mungo was gone!

Lion was lazing in the sun, when Mungo swung down and asked, "Want some fun?" Then he added, "I know a good game."

"Yeah?" said Lion, suspiciously. "What's its name?"

"Funny faces," said Mungo. "What do you say?"

"I don't know how to play," said Lion.

"Easy," said Mungo. "All you have to do is pull a funny face. Look, I'll show you." And he took hold of Lion's bottom lip and pulled it up over Lion's nose. "You see," he said, "that's the way it goes."

Then he ran off through the trees. "Forget what Mum said," thought Mungo. "I'll do as I please." He swung through the branches, but, after a while, Mungo's face lost its smile. "I don't know where I am!" he wailed.

"That's a funny face," said Elephant. "He wins the game for sure."

"It's not a game," howled Mungo. "I'm lost and alone. I want my mum! How do I get out of here? This isn't any fun!"

"Well, shall we help him?" Lion roared. "What do you think?"

"If we do help you, Mungo, then no more funny faces. Do you understand?" the animals asked.

Mungo looked much happier than he'd done in quite a while. "No more tricks!" Mungo promised, and he thanked both of them. "Being lost and alone wasn't any fun for me!"

Thank You Kitty

"Come here, Kitty," calls Cat one day. "You can have lots of fun with this ball of wool." Soon Kitty is laughing and leaping around.

Just then someone calls to her. It's Mother Bird. "Please can I have some of your wool for my nest?" she asks Kitty.

Kitty looks at Cat, and Cat smiles, "It's much more fun to share things, Kitty," she says, "and you have plenty of wool."

Kitty and Cat watch Mother Bird tuck the wool into her nest around her babies. "I like sharing," says Kitty. "Who else can I share with?"

"What about the rabbits?" says Cat.

"We're having a race," says Little Rabbit. "A piece of wool can be a finishing line. Thank you, Kitty."

Just then Cat calls Kitty over. "I have a surprise for you," she says. "It's a bell from Mother Bird," says Cat. "To thank you for sharing your wool."

"What a lovely present," says Kitty. "Would you like to play with it too, Mum?"

You Can Do It Kitty

It's a lovely day. Kitty and Cat are having fun on the farm. "Climbing trees is fun," says Cat. "Watch me, Kitty."

Cat leaps up the tree. "Where are you, Mum?" calls Kitty.

"Climb up, Kitty," calls Cat. "You'll love it up here."

Kitty runs to the tree. But then she starts to cry. "I can't," she sobs. "It's too high."

Cat climbs down and gives Kitty a snuggle. "Don't be upset," she says. "You can do anything you want to do. See that calf? He's trying to walk."

"He cannot even stand up!" says Kitty.

"But very soon he will be able to run," says Cat.

Then Cat climbs the tree again. Kitty takes a deep breath. "Watch me, Mum! I'm going to do it!" she says.

Kitty runs to the tree and jumps! "You've done it, Kitty!" shouts Cat.

Kitty hugs Cat. "It's brilliant up here, Mum," she says. "I can see the whole farm."

Chasing Tails

Barney had been chasing his tail all morning. Round and round he went, until he made himself feel quite dizzy.

"Can't you find something useful to do?" asked the cat, from where she sat watching him on the fence.

Later, trotting round the farmyard, Barney thought about what the cat had said. He wished he could be more useful, but he was only a little pup. When he grew up, he would be a fine, useful farm dog – but then, he rounded the barn, and there in front of him waved a big bushy tail…

"Here's a tail I can catch!" thought Barney playfully, and he sprang forward and sank his sharp little puppy teeth into it!

Now, the tail belonged to a fox, who was about to pounce on Mrs Hen and her chicks! The fox yelped in surprise, and ran away across the fields.

"Barney, you saved us!" cried Mrs Hen.

The cat was watching from the fence. "Maybe all that practice chasing tails has come in useful after all!" she said.

Tiger Tales

Louis and Lisa Lion were just learning to pounce, and their dad had told them to practise as much as they could. So they were prowling through the jungle, looking for prey to pounce upon.

"There's something orange and blue and fluttery," whispered Lisa. "Here I go... " As Lisa pounced on the butterfly, Louis spotted something green and jumpy. He crept up and... POUNCED! As the two little cubs bounded through the jungle, Louis suddenly saw a flash of orange and black in some bushes.

"A stripy snake!" he whispered. "It's too good to pass up!" So, at just the right moment, he... POUNCED!

"Owwww!" came a voice from the bush. "What's got my tail?" The snake turned out to be attached to a stripy cub, just the same size as Louis and Lisa.

"Who are you?" they asked.

"I'm Timmy Tiger," said the little cub. "I've just moved here from The Other Side of the Jungle!"

"We're Louis and Lisa Lion," said Lisa. "Why don't we show you our side of the jungle?"

"Here's our river," said Louis proudly.

"It's nice," said Timmy, "but it's kind of small. Our river on The Other Side of the Jungle is as wide as fifty tall palm trees laid end to end! And I can swim across that river – and back – without stopping once!"

"We can't even swim," said Lisa. "Please will you show us how?"

"Err... maybe another time," said Timmy. "I'm just getting over the sniffles, and Mum said that I shouldn't swim for a while."

A little farther along, Louis and Lisa saw Howard Hippo wallowing merrily in the mud.

"Meet our new friend, Timmy Tiger!" they called.

Howard opened his mouth in a big grin. "Very nice to meet you!" he called.

"Er… same here," said Timmy, keeping his distance.

As the cubs scampered on, Timmy said, "On The Other Side of the Jungle, there's a hippo with a mouth as big as a cave. Three tigers can sit in it!"

As the cubs walked on, something from a branch above dropped down in front of them. Timmy jumped, but Louis and Lisa smiled. "Hi, Seymour! Meet our new friend, Timmy Tiger."

"Greetingssss," hissed Seymour Snake. "Niccce to make your aquaintancccccce!"

"Nice to meet you, too," said Timmy, a little uncertainly. "Well, sssso long," said Seymour, as he slithered off. "Ssssssee you sssssoon I ssuppose!"

As Seymour slithered off, Timmy said, "On The Other Side of the Jungle, there are snakes as thick as tree trunks. Once, one of them swallowed me!"

"Oh, no!" cried Louis and Lisa.

"Yes," Timmy said, "but my dad hit the snake on the head and made him spit me out! My dad's really, really strong, and he's twice as big as an elephant, and he can carry six gorillas on his back! And my mum can stand on her front paws and juggle coconuts with her hind legs, and... "

"... and what?" asked two smiling, normal-sized tigers on the path in front of them.

"... and, here they are," said Timmy, sheepishly. "Mum and Dad, meet my new friends, Louis and Lisa."

"Happy to meet you," said Mr and Mrs Tiger. As you can see," Mrs Tiger added, "we are just very ordinary and normal tigers."

"But what about all those amazing things that Timmy told us?" asked Louis. "And what about The Other Side of the Jungle?"

"It's just like this side," said Mr Tiger.

"So the river isn't as wide as fifty palm trees?" asked Lisa.

"And there's no hippo with a mouth as big as a cave, or a snake who swallowed Timmy?" asked Louis.

"No, indeed!" laughed Mrs Tiger.

Timmy looked embarrassed. "Well, they were good stories," he said.

"Yes," said Mrs Tiger, "but they were just stories." She turned to Louis and Lisa. "Timmy had no friends to play with in our old home, he spent his time imagining amazing adventures."

"But now that he's got friends like you two to play with," said Mr Tiger, "perhaps he'll have some real adventures!"

"And there are more friends to meet, Timmy," Lisa said, "like Mickey and Maxine Monkey, and Chico Chimp!"

"You know, there are monkeys and chimps on The Other Side of the Jungle, too," said Timmy.

"Really?" said Lisa, glancing at her brother.

"Yes," said Timmy, "but I didn't know them. I can't wait to meet Mickey, Maxine and Chico!"

"Well, what are we waiting for?" said Louis, and they all raced off, ready for fun and excitement on This Side of the Jungle.

Chalk and Cheese

Chalk and Cheese were as different as two kittens can be. Chalk was a fluffy white kitten, who liked lazing in the sun. Cheese was a rough, tough black kitten, who liked climbing trees. Their mother puzzled over her odd little pair of kittens, but she loved them both the same.

One day, Cheese got stuck on the barn roof. "Help!" he cried to Chalk.

"I don't like climbing!" she said, from her spot in the sunshine.

"If only you were more like me," said Cheese, "you'd be able to help!"

"If only you were more like me," said Chalk, "you wouldn't have got stuck in the first place!" – and went back to sleep. Just then, the farm dog came by. Chalk sprang up as he gave a loud bark and began to chase her.

"Help!" she cried to Cheese, up on the barn.

"I'm stuck!" he cried. "You shouldn't lie where dogs can chase you!"

Then Mummy appeared. She swiped the dog away with her claws, then climbed up and rescued Cheese.

"If only you were more like me," she said, "you'd keep out of danger and look after each other." And from then on, that's just what they did.

CHALK AND CHEESE

Big Top

It was a grey day in the higgledy-piggledy, messy alley. Harvey and his gang were fed up!

"I'm bored!" moaned Ruffles. "There's nothing to do!"

"What about a game of hide-and-seek?" asked Harvey.

"Boring! Boring!" called Puddles, hanging upside down on the fence.

"What we need is some fun!" yawned Bonnie. "I've got an idea... "

Soon Bonnie and Puddles were jumping on an old mattress. BOINGG! BOINGG! BOINGG! They bounced up and down, up and down.

"This is fun!" shrieked Puddles. "I bet I can bounce the highest."

"I'm the Amazing Bouncing Bonnie," giggled Bonnie. "Look!"

She bounced high into the air – and landed with a thud on a clump of grass!

"Ooops-a-daisy," she said. "I think I missed!"

Then Mac clambered onto the clothesline. "WHEEEE! Look at me! I'm the wibbly wobbly dog."

"Oh no!" gasped Patchy. "Here comes tumble-time," as Mac toppled over onto the mattress below. Mac sat up and rubbed his head, grinning.

Harvey laughed. His friends' tricks had given him an idea.

"Let's put on a circus," he said.

The Alley Dogs all agreed and they scampered off to the playground in search of their big top!

"Okay, everyone," said Harvey, when they arrived. "First, we need to make a circus ring."

"Do you think these old tyres will make good seats?" asked Ruffles.

"They sure will," said Patchy. "And these old plastic bags can be the curtains!" In no time at all, the big top was ready.

"Well done! We must let everyone know that the circus is in town!" said Harvey. "Come on, Ruffles, you've got the loudest voice." So, Ruffles took a deep breath and boomed out loud, "Roll up! Roll up! Come to Harvey's Big Top. See the Greatest Show on Earth!"

Soon the air was filled with woofing and yapping as their pals queued up to see the circus!

The nervous gang huddled behind the curtain.

"Right," said Harvey. "Who's going first?"

Patchy peeped out. "Not me!" she whispered. "There are far too many dogs out there and I'm a bit shy."

"And I'm still practising!" cried Ruffles.

The others shook their heads; no one wanted to go first. They were all scaredy-cats! Harvey crept behind the curtain.

His friends were quivering and quaking. "Silly billies," he smiled. "There's nothing to be scared of. Watch me." He quickly pulled on a cape and ran back into the ring.

"Let the show begin with Harvey the Brave!" he cried, and the audience gave a loud cheer.

"For my first trick," he announced, "the Tricky Tightrope!" He wibbled and wobbled across the top of the swing from one end to the other – and didn't fall off once.

"How does he do it?" gasped the audience, holding their breath in wonder. "Whatever next?" Harvey climbed to the top of a huge pile of bricks.

"Eeek! What if he falls?" squeaked a little dog. "I can't bear to look."

But Harvey made it – and balanced on one paw!

The Alley Dogs peeped out from behind the curtain. Harvey was having such a good time that it didn't look in the least bit scary. So at last, Harvey's Amazing Daring Dogs rushed to join in the fun.

"Look at me," said Ruffles. "I can balance a ball on my tummy."

The audience laughed and cheered and clapped.

Patchy and Mac tumbled and turned on their bouncy mattress – what a pair of clever acrobats!

The show ended with the dangerous and daring Trolley Trick.

Everyone held their breath. Bonnie and Ruffles stood on the bottom, Patchy and Mac climbed onto their shoulders and little Puddles balanced on the very tip-top.

When they were ready, Harvey pushed the trolley round and round the ring.

"More! More!" roared the crowd, as the show came to an end.

"Well, Puddles," smiled Harvey, when they finally got back to their higgledy-piggledy, messy alley, "was that boring, boring, boring?"

"Oh no, Harvey," she said. "It wasn't boring, it was fun, fun, fun!"

Home Sweet Home

Bella Bunny looked at the sweet green grass growing in the meadow on the far side of the stream. She was tired of eating the rough grass that grew near her burrow. "I'm going to cross the stream!" she said to her brothers and sisters, pointing to a fallen branch that lay across it.

Bella bounced safely across the branch and was soon eating the sweet, juicy grass on the other side of the stream. Her brothers and sisters thought she was very brave and wondered if they should follow. But just then, they saw a sly fox creeping up behind Bella through the grass!

"Look out!" they called. Bella turned to see the fox just in time! She leapt back onto the branch, but she was in such a hurry that she slipped and fell into the stream. Luckily, Becky Beaver had been watching and she pulled Bella safely to the other side.

"Home sweet home!" gasped Bella, with relief. And she ran off to join her brothers and sisters, vowing never to leave home again.

Monkey Mayhem

Mickey and Maxine Monkey had finished their breakfast of Mango Munch. Now they were rushing off to play.

"Be careful!" called their mum. "And please DON'T make too much noise!"

"We won't!" the two mischievous monkeys promised, leaping across to the next tree.

"Wheeee," screeched Mickey, and "Wa-hoooo!" hollered Maxine.

The noise echoed through the whole jungle – Mickey and Maxine just didn't know how to be quiet!

Ka-thunk! Mickey landed on a branch. Ka-clunk! Maxine landed beside him. Ker-aack!

"Ooohh noooo!" the monkeys hollered as the branch snapped.

"Yi-i-i-kes!" they shrieked, as they went tumbling down. Ker-thumpp! The jungle shook as the two monkeys crashed to the ground.

"Yipppeeee!" the monkeys cheered, jumping up happily.

"That was so much FUN!" exclaimed Maxine. "Let's go and get Chico Chimp and see if he wants to do it, too!" And the two monkeys scrambled back up to the tree tops, bellowing, "HEY, CHICO! COME AND PLAY WITH US!" as they swung through the branches.

All over the jungle, animals shook their heads and covered their ears. Couldn't anyone keep those naughty, noisy monkeys quiet?

Chico Chimp arrived to play with his friends. The three of them were having a great time swinging, tumbling and bouncing together when suddenly they stopped short. Grandpa Gorilla was standing in their path, glaring at them angrily.

"Go away, you mischief-makers," he said. "You have given us all enough headaches today, and my grandson Gulliver is fast asleep by the river. If you wake him up, I will be very, very upset!"

"Sorry," whispered Maxine, looking down at the ground.

Absolutely everyone in the jungle knew it was a very big mistake to upset Grandpa Gorilla!

"We'll be quiet," they promised.

Mickey, Maxine and Chico didn't know what to do until Mickey said, "Let's climb the coconut palm tree. We can do that quietly."

"Okay," the others agreed half-heartedly.

"I suppose it's better than doing nothing," said Maxine.

From their perch among the coconuts, the three friends could see right over the jungle.

They saw Jerome Giraffe showing his son Jeremy how to choose the juiciest, most tender leaves on a tree… and they saw Portia Parrot giving her daughter Penelope her first flying lesson.

And right down below them, they saw little Gulliver Gorilla sleeping contentedly in the tall grass right beside the edge of the river bank.

And – uh-oh! They saw something else, too… Claudia Crocodile was in the river. She was grinning and snapping her big, sharp teeth – and heading straight for Gulliver!

The friends didn't think twice. Maxine shouted, "GET UP, GULLIVER! GET UP RIGHT NOOOOOOWW!"

Then Mickey and Chico began throwing coconuts at Claudia.

SMACK! they went, right on top of Claudia's hard head.

"OWW-WOOW!" moaned Claudia.

"What's going on here?" Grandpa Gorilla shouted up into the coconut tree. "I thought I told you three to keep quiet!"

All the noise woke Gulliver. The little gorilla sat up, looked around, and ran to his grandpa, who was hurrying towards the river.

When Grandpa saw Claudia he realised what had happened. "I am so glad you're safe!" he said, giving Gulliver a great big gorilla hug. The three monkeys came down from the tree.

"We're sorry we made so much noise," Chico said.

By this time all the gorillas had gathered around, and so had most of the other animals.

"What's going on?" squawked Portia Parrot.

"Yes, what's all the commotion about?" asked Jerome Giraffe.

"These three youngsters are heroes," said Grandpa. "They have saved my grandson from being eaten by Claudia Crocodile!"

"I think you all deserve a reward," said Grandpa. "And I think it should be… "

"Hurrah!" cheered all the other animals and then they held their breath in anticipation.

"… permission to be just as noisy as you like, whenever you like!" Grandpa Gorilla announced.

"YIPPEEE!" cheered Mickey, Maxine and Chico, in their loudest, screechiest voices. Their grins were almost as wide as the river.

"OH, NOOOOO!" all the other animals groaned together – but they were all smiling, too.

One Bad Bunny

Barney was a very bad bunny. He liked playing tricks on his friends. Barney hid Squirrel's nut store, he put sticky honey on Badger's walking stick and Badger was chased by bees, then he put black paint on Mole's glasses, so poor Mole got even more lost than usual!

"It's time we taught that bad bunny a lesson!" said Badger. So, while Barney was sleeping, Mole and Badger dug a big hole. Squirrel fetched some branches to put over the hole and they covered it with grass. They set a big juicy carrot on top, then hid behind the trees to wait.

The next morning, Barney came bouncing out of his burrow, spotted the juicy carrot and jumped straight into the trap!

"Help!" he cried, from the bottom of the hole. The others appeared.

"We tricked you!" they laughed. They only let Barney out when he promised to stop playing tricks on them. And from then on he was a very good bunny indeed.

Don't Be Shy Kitty

Kitty is playing with a yo-yo. "Watch me, Mum," she says. Suddenly, Kitty hears laughing. "What is it, Mum?" she asks Cat.

"The animals are playing a game in the farmyard," says Cat.

"The game is so loud. It makes me feel shy," Kitty says sadly.

"There's no need to be shy," says Cat. "All your friends are there."

"I think I'll just watch them all for a while," says Kitty.

The animals are having a wonderful time. Then, Dennis the donkey gives the ball a big kick. "Does anyone know where the ball is?" asks Dennis.

Quick as a flash, Kitty leaps up and races up the tree. "Here it is!" Kitty laughs, throwing it down from the tree.

"You're a hero, Kitty!" the animals shout. The game starts again and now Kitty is right in the middle of things.

"Great kick, Kitty," shouts Parsnip.

"You were right, Mum," she says. "I didn't need to feel shy at all."

Kitty and Cat Help Out

Kitty and Cat are going for a walk around the farm. Suddenly Cat hears another noise. It's Little Rabbit. "What's the matter, Little Rabbit?" asks Cat. "Why are you crying?"

"I've lost my teddy bear," sniffs Little Rabbit. "It's my favourite toy."

"Don't worry. We'll help you look for it. Perhaps it's behind the haystack, and I'll look inside the tractor," says Kitty.

Cat points to the gate. "Perhaps you left your teddy in the field, Little Rabbit," she says. Little Rabbit begins to cry again.

"Don't give up," says Kitty kindly. "I'm sure we'll find it soon."

"Your teddy could be at home. Have you looked there?" asks Cat.

So they walk to Little Rabbit's home, carefully looking for teddy on the way. But, when they arrive, they find teddy! He is tucked down inside Little Rabbit's bed.

Little Rabbit gives Kitty a big hug. "Thank you, Kitty and Cat," he says. "I'd never have found my teddy without you!"

Hide and Seek

"You can be It, Daisy," said Alex. "You count, and we'll hide."

"Okay," said Daisy. "Poppy can help me to look for you." Poppy was Daisy's new puppy.

"Don't be silly," laughed Sam. "A puppy can't play hide and seek."

"She can because… " began Daisy. But the others weren't listening. They had all run off across the field to hide.

"Never mind, Poppy," Daisy told her puppy. "You'll just have to sit here and be good."

Daisy turned round to face the tree. She closed her eyes and began to count. "… ninety eight, ninety nine, one hundred." That should have given everyone long enough to hide. Daisy looked round the field. There was no one to be seen. Poppy whined as Daisy ran off towards the hole in the hedge where they had made a den.

She found Sam almost straightaway. He was tucked down in a corner of the den. She took him back to the tree. Poppy whined at them.

"Dogs can't play hide and seek," Sam told the puppy, and tickled her ear. "You can sit here with me."

Then Daisy found Sarah and Michael just as easily. Emily was harder to find – she was lying very still in the long grass at the end of the field. Her green T-shirt and trousers made her difficult to see. Daisy took her back to the tree, where the others were all waiting. Poppy whined each time she came back.

"Shhh!" said Daisy. "I won't be long now." But Daisy was wrong – she couldn't find Alex anywhere! Daisy had looked in all their favourite hiding places, but he wasn't in any of them. She didn't know what to do.

"We'll help you to find Alex," said Michael.

So the children searched every corner of the field and every bit of the hedge, but Alex couldn't be found anywhere. Then Poppy began to whine even more loudly.

"She's trying to tell us something," said Daisy. "What is it, Poppy? Show me."

Poppy jumped up. She ran to the tree trunk, leapt up, and began barking. The children all looked up. And there was Alex, sitting on a branch above them, laughing!

"See!" he said. "Daisy was right – puppies can play hide and seek."

Fancy Flying

Penelope Parrot and her mum, Portia, were having a wonderful afternoon, watching the Fancy Flying Display Team. Penelope could hardly believe her eyes as she saw the birds swoop and speed through the sky, doing their amazing tricks and wonderful stunts.

That night, Penelope dreamt about doing magnificent stunts with the other birds and, in the morning, she decided she would try to make her dream come true!

"I'm going to practise flying, Mum," she announced. "I want to be the best!" Before Portia could say a word, Penelope had zoomed off.

"The first thing I have to do is learn to fly really fast," Penelope told herself. So she flapped her wings as hard as she could, to get up some speed. But Penelope had only just learned to fly – so she didn't know how fast or how far she could go. Soon she was huffing and puffing and panting, and her wings were flopping instead of flapping! "Oh, nooooo!" she cried, as she felt herself falling down… down… down… until… SPLASH! She landed right beside Howard Hippo, who had been enjoying his morning wallow. "Gracious, Penelope," said Howard, crossly, as he tried to shake the water out of his eyes and ears. "You must be more careful!"

"Sorry, Howard," said Penelope. "I didn't plan that. I was just seeing how fast I could fly and my wings got tired. I want to be a Fancy Flyer!"

"Then you'll need expert help," said Howard.

"But I don't know any experts," said Penelope.

"But I do," came a voice from the bank.

It was her mum, Portia. "I've been trying to find you to tell you some special news," said her mum. "My uncle Percy has just arrived for a visit. He was a member of the original Fancy Flying team! He can give you the training you need."

Uncle Percy was delighted to hear that Penelope wanted to be a Fancy Flyer. "I'll teach you lots of stunts first," he said, "and then we'll work on one that will be your very own. Every Fancy Flyer has a speciality!"

Uncle Percy and Penelope went right out to start her training programme.

"We'll begin with the Twisting Take Off," Uncle Percy said. "Watch me and do as I do."

"Now, straighten up and fly forward!" Percy called. But Penelope couldn't stop spinning and spinning!

"Whoa!" she shouted. "I'm getting dizzy, Uncle Percy!"

Luckily, Penelope grabbed a branch and managed to stop spinning.

Jeremy Giraffe, who was nibbling leaves nearby, helped Penelope up as Uncle Percy flew back.

"Never mind," said Uncle Percy. "You'll soon get the hang of it."

Just then, Penelope's friends, Mickey, Maxine and Chico, came swinging by.

"Want to play Mango-Catch with us?" they called.

"Great!" said Penelope, flying over to join them.

"Wait!" said Uncle Percy. "A Fancy Flyer in training can't waste her energy on games!"

"Sorry, Uncle Percy," said Penelope. "I guess I'll see you all later," she said, a little sadly.

"In fact," said Uncle Percy, "I think it's time you were in your roost."

"But Uncle Percy," Penelope said, dismayed, "it's so early!"

"A Fancy Flyer needs her sleep, my dear!" said Uncle Percy. "Those wing muscles need lots of rest to prepare for all the work they must do."

"Better do what Uncle Percy says," said Portia, as she helped Penelope settle on to her bedtime branch. "He's the expert!"

The next morning, Uncle Percy woke Penelope up very early. "Time for your pre-dawn practice!" he squawked.

"But Uncle Percy, it's so early!" Penelope yawned. "The sun's not even up yet!"

"That's the best time to train!" said Uncle Percy. "Follow me!"

"We'll start with some speed exercises," Uncle Percy said. "This was my speciality when I was a Fancy Flyer. Just move in and out through the trees – like this!"

Penelope watched her uncle weave gracefully through the jungle. It looked easy, but when she tried...

THUH-WHACK!
"Ouch!" cried Penelope.

Uncle Percy came rushing back to look at Penelope's head.

"Nothing serious," he said. "A Fancy Flyer in training has to expect a few bumps and bruises! Best thing to do is keep going. Let's try it again."

All day, Uncle Percy tried to teach Penelope stunts. And all day, Penelope bashed... and crashed... and smashed... and splashed... into trees and other animals!

It was a very tired and worn-out Penelope who headed for home with Uncle Percy that afternoon.

"Well, Penelope," said Portia, when the two arrived back, "are you ready to be a Fancy Flyer?"

"Oh, yes," said Penelope. "And I know exactly what my speciality will be!"

"What?" asked Portia and Uncle Percy together.

"Watching from the audience!" laughed Penelope.

Polly Piglet's Surprise Party

It was a lovely sunny day but Polly Piglet was feeling sad. "It's my birthday today," she said to herself. "But no one seems to have remembered. Nobody has called to say happy birthday!"

Polly decided to go for a walk. "Maybe my friends will remember if they see me," she told herself and went out into the farmyard.

"There's Holly Horse!" thought Polly. Holly was inside the stables looking very busy. But, as soon as she saw Polly, she stopped what she was doing and began whistling.

"Hello Polly, nice day for a walk!" said Holly.

"Yes it is," said Polly. She waited a minute to see if Holly was going to wish her happy birthday. But Holly just went on whistling.

Just then, five little chicks came rushing past. They looked as if they were on their way somewhere very important. "Hello Polly, we must rush, lots to do, have a nice walk!"

"Everyone's forgotten!" thought Polly crossly. "I was going to make a cake to share with my friends, but now I won't bother."

"There's Lolly Lamb," thought Polly. "She always remembers my birthday!" But, as soon as Lolly saw Polly, she ran off to the barn.

"What is going on?" wondered Polly. But then she saw that Lolly was beckoning Polly to follow her.

A tiny thought crept into Polly's mind, "Mmm, I wonder...?" And off she raced towards the barn, wagging her little curly tail. Dolly Cow was standing at the barn door.

"You've found us at last!" said Dolly smiling, and she stood back to let Polly step inside...

"Happy Birthday, Polly!" shouted Holly Horse, the five little chicks,

Lolly Lamb, Dolly Cow and all of Polly's farmyard friends. "Welcome to your surprise birthday party!"

Mrs Mouse's Holiday

Mrs Mouse was very excited. All year she had been so busy. First there had been nuts and berries to gather in readiness for winter. Then she had needed to give her little house a big spring clean to make it nice and fresh. Now, as the warm sun shone down on the trees and flowers of her woodland home, she had promised herself a well-deserved holiday.

But getting ready for holidays seemed to make one busier than ever! There was so much to do!

First she took out her little case, opened it and placed it carefully on her neatly made bed. Then she rushed to her cupboard and selected some fine holiday dresses. Back to her case she scuttled and laid them in. Now she chose several pairs of shoes – a nice pair of sandals for walking along the front in, a pair of smart shoes for shopping in, an even smarter pair for going to dinner in, and another pair just in case!

"I'll need a couple of sun hats," she thought to herself, and so into the case they went as well. These were followed by a coat, some gloves and a scarf (just in case the breeze got up and it became cold). Then, in case it became very sunny, in went some sunglasses, some sun cream and a sunshade. But, oh dear, there were so many things in the case that it refused to shut. She tried sitting on it, and bouncing on it, but still it stubbornly would not close.

So out from the case came all the things that she had just put in, and Mrs Mouse scurried to the cupboard again and chose an even bigger case. This time they all fitted perfectly, and she shut the case with a big sigh of relief.

Now she was ready to go to the seaside for her holiday. She sat on the train, with her case on the rack above her head, munching her hazelnut sandwiches and looking eagerly out of the window hoping to see the sea. Finally, as the train chuffed around a bend, there it was!

A great, deep blue sea shimmering in the sun, with white gulls soaring over the cliffs and headlands.

"I'm really looking forward to a nice, quiet rest," she said to herself.

Her guesthouse was very comfortable, and so close to the sea that she could smell the clean, salty air whenever she opened her window.

"This is the life," she thought. "Nice and peaceful."

After she had put her clothes away, she put on her little swimming costume and her sun hat and packed her beach bag. Now she was ready for some peaceful sunbathing!

At the beach, she found herself a quiet spot, closed her eyes and was soon fast asleep. But not for long! A family of voles had arrived on the beach, and they weren't trying to have a quiet time at all. The youngsters in the family yelled at the top of their voices, splashed water everywhere, and sent their beach ball tumbling all over Mrs Mouse's neatly laid out beach towel.

Just as Mrs Mouse thought that it couldn't get any noisier, along came a crowd of ferrets. Now if you've ever sat on a beach next to a crowd of ferrets, you'll know what it's like. Their noisy shouting and singing made Mrs Mouse's head buzz.

Mrs Mouse couldn't stand it a moment longer. She was just wondering where she might find some peace and quiet when she spotted a rock just a little way out to sea.

"If I swim out to that rock," she thought, "I will surely have some peace and quiet there." She gathered up her belongings and swam over to the rock. It was a bit lumpy, but at least it was quiet. Soon she was fast asleep again.

Just then the rock started to move slowly out to sea! It wasn't really a rock at all, you see, but a turtle which had been dozing near the surface. Off into the sunset it went, with Mrs Mouse dozing on its back, quite unaware of what was happening.

Eventually, the turtle came to a small, deserted island. At that moment, Mrs Mouse woke up. She looked at the empty beach, and, without even knowing she had been sleeping on a turtle, she jumped off and swam to the shore, thinking it was the beach that she had just left.

Just then, the turtle swam away, and it was then that Mrs Mouse realised what had happened.

For a moment she was horrified. But then she looked at the quiet, palm-fringed beach with no one about but herself, and thought of the noisy beach she had just left.

"Well, perhaps this isn't such a bad place to spend a quiet holiday after all," she thought.

And that's just what she did. Day after day she lazed on her own private beach with no one to disturb her. There were plenty of coconuts and fruits to eat, and she wanted for nothing. She even made herself a cosy bed from palm leaves.

Eventually, though, she started to miss her own little house in the woods and decided it was time to get back home. First she took half a coconut and nibbled out the tasty inside.

"That will make a fine boat for me to sit in," she said.

Next she found a palm leaf and stuck it to the bottom of the shell. She took her little boat to the water's edge and, as the wind caught her palm leaf sail, off she floated back to the boarding house to get her belongings.

As she sailed slowly back she thought, "This is the quietest holiday I've ever had. I may come back here next year!"

Tiger Tricks

Tiger loved to play tricks. Every time he found a new one, he couldn't wait to try it out on all of his friends. His latest one was – tying knots! While Elephant slept, Tiger tied a knot in his trunk! While Monkey dozed, Tiger tied a knot in his tail! While Snake snoozed, Tiger tied *him* in a knot!

Tiger thought it was great fun. The other animals didn't – they were fed up with Tiger, and his tricks.

"I've had enough of this!" said Elephant, rubbing his sore trunk.

"Something has to be done," said Monkey, rubbing his sore tail.

"He's gone too far this time!" said sore Snake.

"We need to catch him before he can try out his tricks on us," said Monkey.

"But that's the problem," said Snake. "We never see him coming in time."

The others agreed. They didn't spot Tiger sneaking up on them because, in the jungle, Tiger's stripes made him really difficult to see! So all the animals thought really hard.

Monkey scratched his head. Snake wriggled and writhed and Elephant swung his trunk.

Suddenly Elephant said, "I've got an idea!" He led them to a fruit tree near the water hole.

Elephant explained his plan, and a huge smile spread across Monkey's face, and Snake began to snigger. Monkey quickly scampered up the tree, and carried down some of the bright red fruits. Snake wriggled around in the earth, until he made a smooth hollow. Then Elephant squeezed the fruits with his trunk, until the bright red juice filled the hollow that Snake had made – and then the animals waited.

It wasn't long before Tiger came strolling along to the water hole, giggling. He started drinking…

Elephant dipped his trunk into the fruit juice and sucked hard. Then he pointed his trunk at Tiger and blew. The juice flew across the clearing, spattering Tiger all over, soaking into his coat. He looked as if he had bright red spots! Tiger jumped with shock.

"Yes, we'll see you coming for miles," said Monkey.

"So you won't be able to sneak up on us and play any more tricks," added Snake.

And all the animals laughed – except for bright red Tiger!

Fire! Fire!

The sun was shining in the higgledy-piggledy, messy alley. "It's much too hot!" Hattie thought to herself, as she tried to find a nice shady spot for a snooze. Her kittens, Lenny and Lulu, were cat-napping under the apple tree and she knew from the loud snoring that Uncle Bertie and Auntie Lucy were fast asleep in their dustbins. Everyone was hiding from the sun – everyone except Cousin Archie!

Archie was lying on top of the fence, slurping his third bottle of milk! He didn't notice the sun's rays shining through the glass of those empty milk bottles. It was focused right onto Hattie's dustbin full of old newspapers – the perfect place for a fire to start!

Suddenly, Hattie's nose twitched. "What's that?" she wondered. "It smells like smoke."

"It is smoke!" she gasped, as she saw bright red and yellow flames leaping out of her dustbin.

"F-Fire!" she cried. "Help!"

"Wake up, Bertie!" cried Hattie. "My dustbin's on fire!"

Uncle Bertie's sleepy head popped up from his dustbin.

"I must have been dreaming, Hattie!" he yawned. "I dreamt that your bin was on fire."

"It wasn't a dream," cried Hattie. "My bin is on fire."

Cousin Archie fell off the fence in shock! He landed right on top of poor Bertie!

"Hurry!" urged Hattie. "We must put the fire out."

All the shouting woke the twins from their dreams.

"Mummy! Mummy!" they meowed, "what's happening?"

Hattie grabbed her kittens and put them on the top of the fence, well away from the dangerous fire.

"You'll be safe here," she told them. Uncle Bertie knew he had to find some water quickly.

"Over there!" Hattie said, pointing to an old bucket by the fence.

"Hooray!" cried Bertie, finding the bucket half full of water. "It might just be enough to put out the fire."

"Cousin Archie!" he cried. "Come and help me."

The two cats ran down the alley, carrying the bucket between them. Then, with smoke billowing all around, Archie and Bertie aimed the bucket of water and let go… SPLOSH! There was a huge sizzling sound.

"Hooray!" Bertie cried, with a sigh of relief. "We've done it!"

But suddenly, a spark from the fire landed on the pile of rubbish next to the dustbin.

"Oh no, we haven't!" wailed Archie. "Now the rubbish is on fire!"

"Quick," Hattie said to Archie. "We need more help. Go and wake up the dogs."

At the other end of the alley, the dogs were all fast asleep.

"Help!" shrieked Archie, as he hurtled towards them. "Hattie's bin is

on fire. It's spreading down the alley and we can't put it out."

But no one stirred. Archie was always playing tricks on the Alley Dogs and today it was just too hot to bother.

Harvey opened one eye lazily.

"That's a good one, Archie," he said. "But you'll have to try harder than that."

"It's true!" Archie shouted, desperately. "Look!"

Harvey sat up slowly. "This had better not be one of your tricks, Archie," he growled. Then he shaded his eyes from the sun and looked up the alley. As soon as he saw the billowing smoke, he knew the Alley Cat was telling the truth.

"Archie's right!" barked Harvey. "Quick, everyone to the rescue!"

The dogs raced up the alley towards the fire. Even little Puddles wanted to help. But Harvey picked her up and put her on the fence by the kittens.

"You can't do a thing, Puddles!" he said. "Just stay here."

The alley was filled with smelly black smoke. All the cats were coughing and choking. But Harvey knew just what to do.

"Quick!" he said. "Everybody to the water-barrel. Use anything you can to gather the water."

Forming a line, the cats and dogs grabbed all the old buckets and cans they could find, while Auntie Lucy stood by the barrel to fill up all the empty containers.

Then, splishing and splashing, they passed the water along the line to Harvey, who threw it over the fire.

Suddenly, Lucy gave a cry. "The water's run out!"

"Oh no!" said Archie. "We'll never put the fire out now."

The Alley Cats and Dogs stared in dismay. What could they do? They must have more water.

"Oh, no! We're going to lose our lovely home," wailed Hattie, bursting into tears.

Suddenly, Lenny had an idea. "I know what to do," he coughed. Grabbing his sister and Puddles, he pulled them over the fence.

"I've just remembered what's in this garden," said Lenny, disappearing into the long grass.

When he came back, he was pulling a hose.

"Mummy!" cried Lenny. "Look what we've got."

Hattie peered through the smoke and gasped. Harvey grabbed the nozzle, as Bertie leapt over the fence and raced to turn on the tap.

With a mighty spurt, the water sploshed out, drenching the blazing boxes and soaking the smouldering bins. Everyone cheered! Some of the water splashed over the cats and dogs – but they didn't care. The fizzling, sizzling fire was out!

"You little ones deserve a treat for saving our alley!" barked Harvey. "Puppy snacks for you, Puddles, and kitty nibbles for the twins."

"Three cheers for Lenny, Lulu and Puddles!" cried Archie.

"Hip-hip-hooray!"

Who's Afraid of...?

The woodland animals were arguing... "I scare everyone when I flutter around," said Bat.

"Rubbish," said Owl. "I'm much scarier than you. You should see animals freeze when I swoop down on them, hooting."

"That's nothing," scoffed Badger. "When I come trundling through the wood, everyone gets out of my way – fast!"

The animals turned to look at Mouse. "You decide," they said. "Tonight, we'll all try to frighten you, and you can judge who is the scariest animal."

"No problem," said Mouse, and he smiled. That evening, Mouse settled down under a tree and waited. Soon, he heard a flapping sound above his head.

"Hi, Bat," he said. "Out for your evening flight, are you?" Bat was surprised that Mouse hadn't been frightened.

"TWIT-TWHOOOO," came an eerie sound from a branch nearby.

Then Owl swept down, staring straight at
Mouse with his piercing eyes.

"I know it's you, Owl," said Mouse.
"You try the same old trick every night."
Owl was amazed that Mouse hadn't
been scared.

Then the ground began to shake and
rumble, and Badger came charging out
of the undergrowth, grunting and growling.

"Really, Badger," said Mouse. "You are so clumsy. You've snapped all
those branches." Badger was stunned that Mouse hadn't been shocked.

"Well, who is the scariest animal in the wood?" asked Bat, Owl and
Badger. "If it's none of us?"

"Well... " said Mouse. "You're not going to believe me but it's..."

Just at that moment, Bat felt something soft brush against his wing.
He began to shiver. Owl felt something dangly touch the top of his head.
He began to tremble. Badger felt something hairy running
along his back. He began to shake.

"Help!" yelled the three animals.

"That," laughed Mouse, "is the scariest animal in the
wood – it's Spider."

The New Arrival

All day long, Old MacDonald's cows grazed in the green meadow and chatted. Nothing happened on the farm that Poppy, Annabel, Emily and Heather didn't know about.

One morning Old MacDonald visited the horses in the field next door.

"Here's an apple for you and George, Tilly," he said. "I wanted you to be the first to hear – we're expecting a new baby on the farm. You can imagine Mrs MacDonald is very excited about it because… "

But, before he could finish, there was the sound of thundering hooves from the field next to them as a cow, bursting with news, dashed off to find her friends.

"Are you sure?" mooed Annabel, as Poppy panted out what she had heard.

"Positive," gasped Poppy.

"Don't you think that Old MacDonald and Mrs MacDonald are a bit old to have a baby?" asked Emily.

"Yes, I thought that," said Poppy. "But I heard it from Old MacDonald himself."

"But if Mrs MacDonald has a baby to look after," said Heather, "who will give me my beauty treatments before the County Show? I simply have to win another rosette this year."

There was complete silence. Then Annabel said what the animals had all been thinking.

"Ladies! This news is far too important for us to keep to ourselves! We must tell the others immediately!" And off the four cows dashed.

So, leaning over the gate, Emily mumbled to Jenny the hen.

"What?" she squawked. "If Mrs MacDonald has a baby to look after, who is going to collect my eggs? I will tell Henry!"

Henry the cockerel crowed when he heard the news. "Well, cock-a-doodle-doo!" he cried. "If Mrs MacDonald has a baby to look after, who will throw me my corn to peck?" So Henry hurried off to talk to Debbie the duck.

And so it went on. Debbie told Milly the cat, who told Percy the pig, who told Bruce the sheepdog. And Bruce scampered off to tell Maria and the rest of the sheep.

By lunch time, all the animals on the farm were feeling very worried.

Things simply wouldn't be the same if Mrs MacDonald was looking after a baby. In fact, the animals were all so busy and bothered, they didn't notice a truck pulling into the farmyard.

"The new arrival!" called Old MacDonald.

"What, already?" squawked Jenny. "But I thought… oh!"

Out of the truck trotted a beautiful little foal, a new friend for Tilly and Old George.

"It's so lovely to have another baby animal on the farm!" cried Mrs MacDonald.

She was too excited to hear the sigh of relief from all the animals, or the mooing from the meadow, as the other cows had a few well-chosen words with Poppy!

Oh, Bear!

Mr Bruin's Big Top Circus

Bear and Rabbit had been shopping. There were posters all over town about the circus that was coming.

"I think I might join the circus," said Bear, as they reached his gate. "I'll walk the tightrope, it's easy peasy." And he leapt on to the clothes line. He began well… he glided gracefully, he somersaulted superbly, he bowed beautifully. Then disaster struck! He wavered and wobbled. He teetered and tottered. He lost his grip and began to slip…

"Oh, Bear!" laughed Rabbit.

"Oh, well," said Bear, as he picked himself up. "Perhaps I'll ride a unicycle instead."

"But you haven't got a unicycle," said Rabbit.

"I can fix that," said Bear. And he disappeared into his shed. Soon, Rabbit heard tools clanging and banging.

"There," called Bear, as he cycled out of the shed. He began quite well. He pedalled up and down. He pirouetted round and round. Then disaster struck!

"Oh, Bear!" laughed Rabbit, as he watched Bear get tangled and the cycle get mangled.

"Oh, well," said Bear. "Perhaps I'll juggle instead."

"But there's nothing to juggle," said Rabbit.

"I'll find something," said Bear. He disappeared into the kitchen. Rabbit waited patiently.

"There," said Bear, as he juggled down the path. He began quite well. He whirled the cups and twirled the plates. Higher and higher they went. Then disaster struck! Everything crashed to the ground with a smash!

"Oh, Bear!" laughed Rabbit.

"I'm not sure the circus is a good idea," Rabbit told Bear.

"Nonsense!" said Bear. "Of course it is."

"But Bear," said Rabbit. "You've tried walking the tightrope, riding a unicycle and juggling. Look what happened!"

"Yes," said Bear. "Look what happened... I made you laugh. Now I know exactly the right job for me," and quickly he ran indoors.

It wasn't long before he was back.

"Oh, Bear!" laughed Rabbit. "You're right. You make a perfect clown!"

Trunk Trouble

Emma, Ellen and Eric Elephant had spent nearly all day at the river, splashing and sploshing in the cool, clear water and giving each other excellent elephant showers. But now it was nearly dinner time, and their rumbling tummies told them it was time to head for home.

First the little elephants had to dry themselves off. They made their way out to the clearing, and carefully dusted themselves with fine earth and sand. WHOOSH! WHOOSH! PUFFLE! went Ellen and Emma with their trunks. Both sisters had long, graceful trunks, and they were very proud of them. WHOOSH! PUFFLE! WHOOSH PUFF! went Eric, when his sisters' backs were turned. COUGH! COUGH! AH-CHOO! went Emma and Ellen.

"Hey! Cut it out!" they shouted.

Eric giggled – he loved annoying his sisters. "I'll race you home!" Eric called. "Last one back is an elephant egg!" as he loped off to the jungle.

Ellen and Emma ran after him. "We'll get there first! We'll beat you!" they cried, going as quickly as they could. Ellen and Emma were running so fast and trying so hard to catch up that they forgot to look where they were going. All at once, Emma's feet got tangled up in a vine, and she lost her balance.

"Oh-oh-OOOOHHHH!" she cried as she slipped, wobbled and staggered.

"Grab hold of my trunk!" Ellen cried, reaching out. But Emma grabbed her sister's trunk so hard that she pulled Ellen down with her and their trunks got twisted together in a great big tangle.

"Help!" they cried. "Eric! Help!" Their brother came bounding back.

"Don't worry!" he called. "I'll save you both!"

Eric reached out with his trunk to try to help his sisters up. But the vine leaves were very slippery, and, as he grabbed his sisters' trunks, he slipped and then he lost his balance!

Now Eric's trunk was all tangled up with Emma's and Ellen's! The three elephants sat there in a sad, tangled heap. They could barely move.

"What are we going to do?" wailed Emma.

"Don't worry, someone will come and help us," Ellen said, hopefully.

"This is all your fault!" Eric grumbled. "If it wasn't for you two, I'd be home now, eating my dinner!"

A moment later, Seymour Snake came slithering by. "Isss thisss an interesting new game?" he hissed, looking at the heap of elephants.

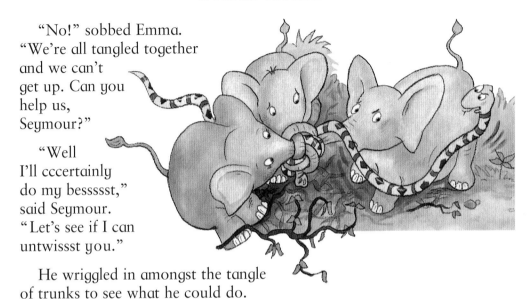

"No!" sobbed Emma. "We're all tangled together and we can't get up. Can you help us, Seymour?"

"Well I'll cccertainly do my bessssst," said Seymour. "Let's see if I can untwissst you."

He wriggled in amongst the tangle of trunks to see what he could do.

But everything was so muddled and jumbled together that Seymour couldn't even find his way out! "GRACIOUSSS ME!" he exclaimed. "I SSSEEM TO BE SSSSTUCK!"

"Great!" said Eric. "Now we have a snake to worry about, too!"

"I ssssuggest you sssstart thinking about a ssssolution to all thissss," Seymour hissed. "I'm not too tangled up to give you a nasssty nip!"

Just then Mickey and Maxine Monkey swung through the branches.

"HEY, YOU GUYS!" they shouted.

They weren't very far away – Mickey and Maxine always shouted. "WHAT'S GOING ON?"

"We're stuck!" cried Ellen. "Please untangle us so we can go home!"

"Well, we can try pulling you apart," said Maxine, scurrying down. "Mickey, you take a tail, and I'll take some ears."

Mickey grabbed hold of Eric's tail and Maxine gripped Ellen's ears. Then they both pulled and pulled and p-u-l-l-e-d.

"OUCH-OUCH-OUUCCH-OOUUCCHH!" bellowed Ellen. "I'm being ssssqueezzzed breathlesssss!" hissed Seymour in alarm.

Mickey and Maxine gave up. Pulling clearly wasn't going to work at all.

Suddenly there was a flapping up above as Portia Parrot and her daughter Penelope flew above with something in their beaks. As everyone looked up, they let it go and a large cloud of dry, dusty, earth drifted downwards.

"Cough-cough-ca-choooo!" spluttered Mickey and Maxine.

"Cough-cough-ca-choooo!" thundered the elephants. At first, they didn't know what had happened. Then they realised – they had sneezed themselves apart!

"Thank you," cried the elephants and Seymour.

"Happy to help!" said Portia.

"Everyone's invited to our house for dinner!" said Eric.

"Hooray!" cried the others.

With their trunks held high, the elephants led the way – walking calmly and very, very carefully!

Not Another Bear

William loved teddy bears, he always asked for a teddy for his birthday, or for Christmas.

"Not another bear!" his parents would say. "Look at your bed, William. There's no room for more!" There were so many bears on William's bed that William had to squeeze into the tiny space that was left!

"We've got to do something about this," said William's dad. "We'll make some shelves, so that you can have some room." By tea time there were three shelves on William's bedroom wall with a row of bears on each one. There was plenty of room in bed for William, but it didn't feel right.

Next day, at the school fair, Mum gave William some pocket money. William bought a small bear on the White Elephant stall and when they got home he ran straight upstairs.

"What did you buy, William? Oh no! Not another bear!" sighed Mum.

"But there's plenty of room now," William answered. He winked at the new bear, and William was sure that the bear winked back.

Yes, You Can!

Ozzie sat on the river bank watching the other otters. He wished he could splash in the water like them. But Ozzie couldn't swim!

"What's the matter, Ozzie?" asked his mum.

"I wish I could swim so I could have fun with my friends," said Ozzie.

"But you can," laughed Mum. "Climb on my back and hold tight." So, with Ozzie holding on to his mum's back, they swam round in small circles. At first, Ozzie was frightened. Then, he began to enjoy the water.

"This is fun! Can we do it again?" he cried. But there was no answer. Ozzie's mum wasn't there. She was on the river bank, smiling at him.

"Don't panic!" called his mum. "Pretend you're running!" Suddenly, he felt himself swimming! Round and round he went, splashing and diving.

On the bank, he found a tiny otter shivering. "What's the matter?" asked Ozzie.

"I can't swim," said the otter.

"Come on, climb on my back and I'll show you!" smiled Ozzie, happily.

Grandma Elephant's Birthday

"Boris," said his parents, "it's a special day today. Can you remember why?" They say elephants never forget, but Boris never remembered.

"Do I start school today?" he said. "Or perhaps it's my birthday?" asked Boris.

"Getting closer," said Mum. "It's Grandma Elephant's birthday! I want you to take her this basket of fruit. Can you remember where she lives?"

"Yes," nodded Boris. Mum gave him the basket and off he went.

The path was very narrow. Right in the middle, blocking the way, was a huge gorilla.

"I'm taking fruit to Grandma," said Boris bravely. "It's her birthday."

"Don't you remember who I am?" asked Gorilla.

"You're Rhinoceros," Boris guessed.

"If you can't remember who I am," said Gorilla, "you'll have to give me some fruit!"

Boris didn't remember, so Gorilla took two bananas and let Boris pass.

Reaching a crossroads, Boris wasn't sure which path to take. "Take the left path," said a voice high above him. Looking up, Boris saw Giraffe's head sticking out of the top of a tree. "Are you going to Grandma Elephant's? I can see her house from up here," said Giraffe.

"Thank you," said Boris. "Have some fruit!"

"That's very kind of you," said Giraffe. He took a pear from the basket.

When Boris arrived at Grandma's house, all that was left in the basket was one juicy plum! Would Grandma be cross? He needn't have worried. Grandma hugged him and took him to the kitchen.

There, sitting round the table, were Gorilla and Giraffe. In the middle of the table was a big birthday cake, a large wobbly red jelly, and all the fruit from Boris's basket! They had a wonderful party.

Boris couldn't remember the way home. So when the party was over his friends took him all the way back, and Boris introduced them to Mum.

"These are my friends, Crocodile and Rhinoceros," said Boris.

Everybody laughed. Silly Boris... what a memory!

Billy Bunny's Shopping List

Billy Bunny wanted to play, but Mummy needed his help. "You can tidy the burrow or you can do the shopping," she said. Billy knew that if he went shopping he might see his friends on the way. "I'll do the shopping," he said. Mummy gave him a list which read: five acorns, two carrots and some parsley.

As Billy went skipping through the woods, a gust of wind blew the list out of his paw and it floated away. "Never mind," said Billy. "I'm sure I'll remember everything!"

But he couldn't remember anything. He met his friend Fox, who said, "Get some flowers. Mummies always like flowers." So Fox and Billy Bunny picked a few bluebells that grew beside the stream.

"What else?" said Billy. "I know – I'll ask Dora Deer." Dora Deer was playing a leaping game near the fallen logs. Billy and Fox joined in, but after a while Billy remembered the shopping.

"If your mummy had written a list, what would be on it?" Billy asked. Dora thought hard for a minute. "Leaves," she said at last. "Lots of nice fresh leaves to make my bed soft. I'm sure leaves were on your list."

Owl watched them gather a basket of leaves. "I know what your mummy wants," she said, blinking wisely. "All mummies like it when their friends come to visit. I bet your list said 'Invite all my friends to tea'."

"Are you sure?" asked Billy. "I think I would have remembered that." Owl just sniffed and said, "We owls know everything." So Billy ran around the woods and invited everyone he knew to come to tea that afternoon.

Billy went home with flowers and leaves.

"Don't worry," he told his mummy. "I lost your list, but I remembered everything – and everyone is coming to tea this afternoon!" Mummy Bunny didn't have time to be cross – she had far too much to do!

Her friend Moose brought some berry cakes and, by the time everyone arrived for tea, Mummy had almost forgiven her silly Billy Bunny!

Troublesome Sister

In the higgledy-piggledy, messy alley it was tidy-up time! Harvey and the gang had worked hard all morning, scribbling and scrabbling in the heaps of junk trying to clean up their home.

At last, the skip was full of rubbish and they could have a break. All the gang settled down for a snooze, except for Puddles, Harvey's little sister.

"Where's my teddy?" she wondered. "And where's my ish?" Puddles' 'ish' was a blanket she'd had since she was a baby. It was full of holes and rather smelly, but she loved it lots.

She looked round the alley. "Teddy! Ish!" she called. "Where are you?" She didn't see them peeping out from the top of the skip.

Puddles was always getting into lots of mischief and today she scampered off down the alley, sure that she would find her teddy and ish down there somewhere. Spotting a hole in the fence, she peeped through and saw an old box of toys. "Are teddy and ish in there?" she wondered.

She squeezed and squashed herself through the gap and crept up to the toybox.

"Teddy! Ish! Are you in there?" she called. But they weren't. She did find an old toy mouse, hidden away at the back. "Doesn't anyone love you?" she asked. "You're very soft and cuddly – I'll love you! Come on, Mousey," she giggled. "You come home with me." Puddles was feeling much happier.

But Lulu the kitten wasn't. The mouse was her favourite toy and as Puddles trotted off she began to wail.

"Mummy! Mummy! Come quickly!" she cried.

Hattie, Lulu's mum, appeared through a gap in the fence. "What a terrible noise you're making," she purred. "What is the matter?"

Lulu sobbed and sniffed. "Mummy! Puddles has taken my Mousey!" cried the kitten.

"There, there," purred Hattie, trying to stop the sobs. "Don't you worry, Lulu, we'll soon get Mousey back."

But Lulu just screamed even louder.

Puddles didn't hear poor Lulu crying. She was dancing around the garden with her new friend. "We are having fun, aren't we, Mousey!" she laughed as she skipped along. "Now all I need is an ish."

As she skipped through the garden next door, Puddles saw a tatty, old scarf hanging down from the branch of an apple tree.

"Oh look, Mousey!" she cried. "A cuddly ish with no one to love it."

"Well, it's not really an ish," she thought, "but it is very, very soft." She reached up and took one end in her mouth. With a pull and a tug, the scarf floated down. Puddles picked it up and cuddled it. Now she was really happy. She didn't see Lenny, Lulu's brother, fast asleep in the flowerbed nearby.

Lenny woke up with a start and suddenly saw Puddles skipping off along the garden with his favourite scarf – the one he had hung in the tree to use as a swing! He couldn't believe his eyes and began to cry.

"Mummy! Mummy!" he wailed, loudly.

Hattie and Lulu squeezed through the hedge.

"That naughty Puddles has stolen my scarf," sobbed Lenny.

Hattie sighed. Oh dear, now both her twins were crying. Something would have to be done about that pup!

Just then, Puddles popped through the hedge and ran straight into the angry Alley Cats.

"Oh no!" gulped Puddles. "Someone's in trouble, and I think it's me!"

Lulu and Lenny were hiding behind Hattie who looked very cross. Puddles was suddenly scared and she began to cry. "H-H-Harvey!" she croaked. "Help me!"

Puddles' wailing woke up Harvey and the gang.

"Is that Puddles I can hear?" said Ruffles. "Yes! Run, Harvey, run! Puddles needs your help!"

"Hang on, Puddles," woofed Harvey. "I'm coming!" And off he ran, as fast as he could go…

Harvey burst through the hedge. "Okay, guys!" he gasped. "What's all this fuss about?"

The angry Alley Cats began shouting all at once. Puddles hid behind her big brother and shivered and shook. Whatever had she done?

There was so much noise that Harvey couldn't hear a word that anyone was saying.

"QUIET!" he barked. And they were – even the kittens!

"Thank you," said Harvey. "Hattie, tell me, what is all the noise about?"

"That scallywag sister of yours has stolen my twins' favourite toys," grumbled Hattie.

"Well did you, Puddles?" asked Harvey.

"Well, I didn't mean to, Harvey," she cried. "I thought that no one wanted them."

She gave back little Mousey and the tattered and torn scarf.

"Sorry, Lulu," she whimpered. "I am sorry, Lenny. I only wanted to love them."

"Okay, Puddles," smiled the twins. "But you see, we love them too!"

Hattie looked at Puddles and shook her head, she really was an annoying puppy. Harvey gave a huge sigh – panic over!

"Puddles, you're such a scamp," smiled Harvey.

"But I was only looking for my teddy and my ish," cried Puddles. "I don't know where they are."

"Oh, is that what this is all about?" said Harvey.

He scooped them from the skip and gave them back to Puddles with a hug and a kiss. "Now, no more trouble today," he said. "Let's all have a dog-nap."

Puddles hugged her teddy and stroked her ish; she was happy again. "Well," said Puddles, looking at Harvey with a naughty grin, "Ish and I will be good, but Teddy might not!"

Horse Power

On the day of the County Show, there was hustling and bustling on the farm. Mrs MacDonald had to feed the animals and collect the eggs by herself, because Old MacDonald was busy cleaning his tractor.

Every year, Old MacDonald gave rides on his tractor and trailer to the children. They loved it, but it was a lot of hard work for the farmer, with wheels to wash, and paintwork to polish.

At last, the tractor was spotlessly clean. But, when Old MacDonald turned the key, there was silence. The tractor simply would not start. Old MacDonald tweaked the engine – and got his hands greasy.

He stamped and stomped, he muttered and moaned but none of it did any good. The tractor didn't cough or splutter or show any sign of life.

"I hate to let the children down," groaned Old MacDonald. "But I can't pull the trailer without a tractor."

Now, Henry the cockerel sometimes has good ideas. He jumped up on to Old George and Tilly's stable door and gave his loudest, "Cock-a-doodle-doo!"

Old MacDonald gave a big smile. "Goodness, gracious me!" he cried. "You're right, Henry – horse power! Now quick, jump out of the way. There's lots of work to be done!"

There were tails to untangle, coats to comb, and manes to thread with ribbons. There were harnesses to hitch and reins to clean and hang with gleaming brasses.

"It's just like the good old days," neighed Old George to Tilly.

There was no doubt who the stars of the County Show were that year. Old George and Tilly plodded proudly up and down with their coats shining and their heads held high.

At the end of the afternoon, Old MacDonald led the horses home and gave them a special supper of apples and oats.

"You know," he said with a sigh as he stroked their manes, "I miss the old days, too."

Old George and Tilly nodded their great heads, but it wasn't to show they agreed with him. They were asleep on their feet – they're not as young as they used to be, and it had been a very busy day!

Snap Happy

One lazy morning, Claudia Crocodile was drifting down the river, looking for fun. Up ahead, she could see Mickey and Maxine Monkey and Chico Chimp playing on the riverbank.

"I think I'll give them a fright," decided Claudia. "It's always amusing to watch them run away!"

Flashing and gnashing her sharp teeth, she swam towards the three friends. Sure enough, the SNAP! SNAP! SNAP! of Claudia's jaws scared the little monkeys.

"RUN," cried Maxine, "before she snaps our tails off!"

They tumbled over each other as they climbed to safety.

"Hee, hee!" Claudia laughed as she watched them. "Scaring the monkeys is such fun!"

That afternoon, Claudia was bored again, so she looked for someone else to frighten. "Aha!" she said. "There's little Timmy Tiger, paddling all by himself. I'll give him a real fright!"

And she set off down the river, SNAP-SNAP-SNAPPING as she went.

Timmy didn't hear Claudia, until she was right behind him! SNAP! SNAP! went her great big jaws. GNASH! GNASH! GNASH! went her sharp, pointy teeth.

"AAAAGGGGGHHH!" screamed Timmy, as he saw Claudia's mouth open wide. He tried to run away, but his paws were stuck in the mud!

Claudia came closer and closer. Timmy trembled with terror.

"You're supposed to run away!" Claudia whispered.

"I c-c-can't," stammered Timmy. "I'm stuck!"

"Oh," said Claudia, disappointed. "It's no fun if you don't run away."

"Aren't you g-going to eat me?" gulped Timmy.

"EAT YOU?" roared Claudia. "Yuck! You're all furry! I prefer fish."

"Really?" said Timmy. "Then why are you always snapping and gnashing and frightening everyone?"

"Because that's what crocodiles do!" said Claudia. "We're supposed to be scary. Er... you won't tell anyone I didn't eat you, will you?" she asked, helping Timmy climb out of the mud.

"Don't worry," laughed Timmy, "I won't tell!"

"Thanks very much for un-sticking me," Timmy said. "I never knew you could be nice. I like you!"

Claudia's green face blushed bright red!

"I think everyone would like you," went on Timmy, "if you just tried to be friendly, instead of scary."

"Oh, I don't think I can do that," said Claudia. "My jaws simply HAVE to snap and my teeth just MUST gnash! I can't help it."

"Wait!" said Timmy. "I know just how you can be friendly and helpful and snap and gnash at the same time! Here's your chance."

As Timmy and Claudia went along together, they saw Mickey and Maxine trying to smash open some coconuts.

Claudia swam towards the monkeys, SNAP-SNAP-SNAPPING with her jaws. When they heard her, the monkeys ran up the nearest tree.

"I just want to help," said Claudia, climbing on to the bank. "Throw me a coconut!" And with a SNAP! SNAP! SNAP! quick as a flash, Mickey's coconut was open. Then Claudia opened Maxine's coconut, too, and soon everyone was sharing the cool, refreshing milk and chewy chunks of coconut. Claudia had never shared anything and found that she liked it!

Chico Chimp came running towards his friends. He was carrying a huge watermelon. Suddenly, Chico spotted Claudia, whose jaw was open, ready to SNAP! "Uh-oh!" he gulped, turning to run.

"Don't worry, Chico," said Maxine. "Throw Claudia the watermelon!"

Chico watched in amazement as Claudia SNAP-SNAP-SNAPPED the watermelon into neat slices for everyone. "Thanks, Claudia!" they all chorused. Chico gave Claudia the biggest slice.

Then Emma, Eric and Ellen Elephant came trundling down to the river with bundles of thick branches in their trunks. "We're going to make a raft!" said Emma – and then they saw Claudia.

As the frightened elephants galloped away, Claudia picked up the branches they had dropped. SNAP! SNAP! GNASH! GNASH! went Claudia's strong jaws and sharp teeth.

"Wow! Thanks, Claudia!" said Emma, as the elephants came back. "That was really helpful!"

Claudia grinned. Being friendly and helpful was rather nice!

"Here we go!" shouted the elephants, when their raft was ready. The friends on the riverbank watched them.

"That looks like so much fun!" said Chico. "Can you help us make a raft, too, Claudia?"

"I can do even better," said Claudia. "Hop on my back!"

"WHEEE! This is GREAT!" whooped Maxine as they all sailed down the river on Claudia's back.

Happiest of all was Claudia, who had found that having friends was much more fun than scaring them!

Aunty and the Flowers

Every year on the farm, the animals had a competition. Everyone joined in the fun, and there was a prize for the winner. The prize could be for anything. One year it was for growing the best purple vegetables. Once it was for the knobbliest knees. (Gladys the duck won that, of course.)

This year they decided the prize would be for the best display of flowers. But who should be the judge? If Nelly the hen were the judge, she would make herself the winner. She always did. Blink the pig covered everything in mud and Rambo the horse was too big to get in the tent! But Aunty the goat wanted the job. She told the others how much she liked flowers. So why not? Aunty had never been a judge before and so she was chosen.

The big day came. Everyone had been busy for days. The tent was full of flowers, colour and light. Perfect! The judge, Aunty, came in first. She looked very important and was taken to the first display made by Bramble the sheep.

"So I just have to choose which flowers I like best?" Aunty asked.

"Whichever display you think is best wins the prize. This is Bramble's display. He has spent all morning getting it right," said Blink the pig.

"It's called 'Daisies and Dandelions'," said Bramble proudly. The flowers were white and yellow and looked very pretty in a blue mug. Aunty looked at them carefully. She sniffed them. And then she ate them. The others were so surprised, that they couldn't speak! They just stared as Aunty went to the next one, "Buttercups and Roses". She ate them too! Then the goat tilted her head back, half closed her eyes in a thoughtful way, and compared "Buttercups and Roses" with "Daisies and Dandelions". Then, moving along the line, she ate "Cowslips and Honeysuckle", then she ate "Chrysanthemums and Poppies"!

Aunty wrinkled up her nose. "Bit sour, that," she said. Then she turned and saw all the others looking at her with their mouths open. She looked from one to the other, red poppies drooping from the sides of her mouth.

"What?" she said, puzzled. "What!"

Everyone burst out laughing, then they explained it all to Aunty. She thought the whole idea of looking at flowers was very odd, she didn't know that people did that!

There was no time to pick more flowers and start again. Instead, they gave Bramble the prize... Aunty had decided that Bramble's flowers tasted the best!

At the end, the judge is always given a bunch of flowers as a small, thankyou gift. Aunty was very pleased... She ate it!

The Cow who Jumped Over the Moon

Boing, boing, boing! Bouncy Bunny kicked up her heels and bounded happily across the field.

"I can bounce high in the air, watch me!" she called to the other animals on the farm. Her fluffy white tail bobbed up and down.

"Very good!" said Silly Sheep, who was easily impressed.

"Yes, very good," said Swift the sheepdog. "But not as good as me. I can jump right over the gate."

With that, he leapt over the gate and into the field.

"Amazing!" said Silly Sheep.

"Yes, amazing," said Harry Horse, with a flick of his mane. "But not as amazing as me. I can jump right over that hedge. Watch me!" And with that, he galloped around the field, then leapt high into the air, and sailed over the tall hedge.

"Unbelievable!" said Silly Sheep.

"Yes, unbelievable," said Daisy the cow, chewing lazily on a clump of grass. "But not as unbelievable as me. I can jump over the moon!"

"Well, I'm afraid that is unbelievable, Daisy," said Harry Horse. "No one can jump over the moon. That's just a fairy story."

"Well, I can," said Daisy, stubbornly. "And I can prove it! You can watch me do it if you like!"

The other animals all agreed that they would very much like to see Daisy jump over the moon.

"Meet me here, in the field in the middle of the night, then," said Daisy to them. "When the moon is bright and full, and all the stars are bright."

So later that night, when the moon had risen high up in the sky, the excited animals gathered together in the field. The rest of the animals from the farm came along too, for word had soon spread that Daisy the cow was going to jump over the moon, and they were all eager to watch.

"Come along then, Daisy," said Swift the sheepdog, as the animals waited impatiently. "Are you going to show us how you can jump over the moon or not?"

All the animals laughed because they thought that Daisy was just boasting, and that she would not really be able to do it.

"Yes, I am going to show you," said Daisy, "but, first of all, you will have to come with me. This isn't the right spot." Daisy led the animals across the field, to the far side, where a little stream ran along the edge of the field, separating it from the dark woods on the other side. As they crossed the field, they looked up at the great, yellow moon shining down on them. It looked so very far away. However did Daisy think that she could jump so high?

"Now, stand back everyone, and give me some room," said Daisy. The animals did as they were asked, and watched Daisy with anticipation, giggling nervously. Whatever was she going to do?

Daisy trotted back to the middle of the field, turned, then stopped, shuffling backwards and forwards as she took up her starting position.

"Come on, Daisy," cried the animals, impatiently. Daisy took a deep breath, then ran towards the stream at a great speed.

At the very last moment, she sprang into the air, and sailed across the stream, landing safely on the other side of the water.

"I did it!" cried Daisy. "Aren't you going to clap, then?" The other animals looked at each other in confusion.

"But you only jumped over the stream!" said Harry Horse, puzzled.

"Come and take a closer look," called Daisy, still on the far side. The animals gathered close to the water's edge. They looked down, and there reflected in the water, shimmered the great full moon! How the animals laughed when they realised Daisy had tricked them.

"See?" said Daisy. "I really can jump over the moon!" And, just to prove that she really could, she jumped back to the field again. All the animals all clapped and cheered.

"That was a very good trick!" said Swift the sheepdog.

"Amazing!" said Silly Sheep. "Could someone explain it to me again, please?"

The
New Cat

The cats on Old MacDonald's farm like nothing better than dozing. Milly just loves to laze in the sun, and Lazy, as his name suggests, hardly opens his eyes!

One day, Milly was snoozing on a bale of hay, when she heard Old MacDonald talking on the telephone through the open kitchen window. Half-asleep, she heard him say, "The new cat... " Milly was feeling very sleepy. "Yes," continued Old MacDonald, "I need it because the ones I have now are useless."

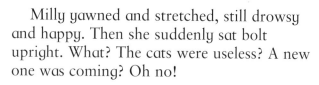

Milly yawned and stretched, still drowsy and happy. Then she suddenly sat bolt upright. What? The cats were useless? A new one was coming? Oh no!

Milly dashed to where Lazy was fast asleep and eventually woke him up! She hurriedly shouted what she had heard.

"What's the matter with us?" yawned Lazy in a hurt voice. "I don't understand."

"You don't do anything," clucked Henrietta the hen, who liked to put her beak into everybody's business. "You just sleep all day."

Milly and Lazy looked at each other. They knew there was only one thing to do. Ten seconds later, they were tearing around the farmyard, trying to look as busy as possible!

By the end of a week of dashing around all day and miaowing all night, the cats had created quite a stir in the farmyard.

"Look here," said Bruce the sheepdog. "What has got into the two of you?"

Milly and Lazy explained. Bruce tried not to smile. "Well, you're doing the right thing," he barked. "Impress Old MacDonald like this and you'll be fine. But I would stop the caterwauling at night."

Bruce strolled off chuckling to himself. As Old MacDonald's right-hand dog, he knew that the farmer was waiting for a new CATalogue to order his winter wellies from. But he didn't think he needed to tell Milly and Lazy that – not quite yet anyway!

Who Can Save the Chicks?

One morning on Windy Farm, three naughty chicks escaped from their hen house and waddled into the farmyard. "Yippeeeeee!" they cheeped, noisily. "I know that Mummy said we weren't allowed outside the hen house by ourselves," cheeped Chalky Chick, "but there's nothing to do inside! Let's go to the river and play."

"That's a great idea!" cried the other chicks. What fun the chicks had, down by the river. But, as the chicks had fun, they didn't realise that danger was nearby!

Wicked Fox was hiding behind the tree. "Lunch!" he murmured.

"I'm going to get them!"

Luckily, up in the tree, Owl had woken and, spotting Fox, he flew off to the farm for help. But all the other animals were out searching for the missing chicks. Only Pig was left.

"Quickly," cried Owl to Pig. "Fox is going to eat the chicks!"

Pig got up and ran after Owl, as fast as he could. Once Pig got moving, there was no stopping him! He reached the river in no time at all and, as he staggered to a halt, he crashed into that nasty Fox, tossing him into the water with a big, loud SPLASH!

The chicks were very surprised by the sudden arrival of Pig and Owl, and even more shocked to see how close to them Fox had been.

"Everyone was worried about you," said Pig to the little chicks, sternly.

"We're sorry!" cheeped the chicks. "We won't do it again – but getting wet was fun!" And Pig and the chicks dripped all the way back home!

Honey Bear
and the Bees

One day, as Honey Bear woke from her dreams, her furry little nose started to twitch with excitement. She could smell her most favourite thing in the world – sweet, yummy honey! It was coming from a hollow tree stump nearby. She padded over and dipped in a large paw. How delicious the sweet, sticky honey tasted! Honey Bear dipped her paw in again and again, digging deep into the tree stump to reach more of the lovely, sticky honey. This was the life! In fact, she dug so deep that, when she tried to take her great paw out, she found it was stuck fast!

Just then, she heard a loud buzzing noise and looked up to see a huge swarm of angry bees returning to their hive! Poor Honey Bear hollered as the bees flew around, stinging her all over! She tugged and tugged and at last she pulled her paw free. The angry bees chased her all the way to the river where she sat cooling her burning skin.

But then an irresistible smell reached her furry nose. It was coming from a hollow tree nearby. "Mmm, honey!" said Honey Bear. "I'll just go and take a look… "